BRO

I came to Kef
no one was at the s
an hour, but still n
stationmaster how I could get to the camp, to Kefferstadt. He told me that it was down a road to the east.

It was early autumn and the weather was still warm so I started walking, my bag perched on my shoulder. As I walked, the fields gave way to a small forest. It was beautiful with the leaves turning color, all golden and red. One would never have known there was a war on.

After a while, a farm cart pulled by a skinny nag came along and the driver let me ride with him. The man was thin and bent, wisps of gray hair peeking out from under a battered hat. When I told him my destination, he shook his head and muttered something I didn't quite understand, something about an abattoir and hell. I never guessed then how my life was about to change forever.

Years after the end of WWII, when the two brothers Hans and Herschel Rothberg have passed on, a lawyer presents their surviving family with a letter, a document that turns their world completely upside down. This manuscript chronicles the relationship of two young men, boys actually, who are thrown together by their experiences in a Nazi concentration camp. It describes their amazing journey from the horrors of Kefferstadt to a displaced persons camp in Germany, and finally to the United States.

Herschel and Hans Rothberg were brothers in the truest sense of the word. Separately, they were doomed, but if they could find a way to work together, they just might be able to survive.

Early Reviews:

"I held my breath reading until the end! I absolutely could not put down this book until I found out what was going to happen to Herschel and Hans."
J.M. Bolton author of "Alien Within"

"It's so real, you feel like you're actually there! What a great adventure. You couldn't find two more unlikely allies, and yet Kafrissen makes it work!"
Marlene A Becker author of "The Deacon & the Demon"

"Brothers Beyond Blood tells the story of two German teen-aged boys enduring the horror of a World War II concentration camp, one a detainee and the other a guard. Their friendship becomes their redemption during the final days of the Nazi regime. This is a must for young adult readers who will form an instant bond with the boys and their victory over evil."
Jerry Cowling, author of "Lincoln in the Basement"

Also by
Don Kafrissen

Missing Pieces
White Emeralds
Mustang Charlie
Gunfight on Clearwater Beach
Short Story Collection
On Top of Her Game
The Brooksville Terrorist
MOSAIC 2010

Brothers Beyond Blood

Don Kafrissen

International Digital Book Publishing Industries
FLORIDA, USA

For information visit our website at
www.idbpi.wordpress.com

ISBN 978-1-57550-035-5

Digital Books are published by International Digital Book Publishing Industries
Brooksville, Florida 34601.

PRINTED IN THE UNITED STATES OF AMERICA

10 9 8 7 6 5 4 3 2

This book is dedicated to the members of the Brooksville Writers' Group;

Jerry, Johanna, Marlene, John, Linda, Karen, Judy, Dennis, Christine, Debbie, Mary, Cynthia, Mike, Charlotte, and Al & Jill, my bro Sam and to

Diane, my wife, and best friend.

And to George Kirshey, owner of Luigi's Pizza, the gathering spot for our Tuesday morning philosophical breakfasts.

Many thanks to my editor, Jill Svoboda, for the hours she put into the forlorn attempt to make me a better writer.

To my good friend, Johanna M. Bolton, a noted writer in her own right, for her encouragement and suggestions.

BROTHERS BEYOND BLOOD

A book from IDBPI published by arrangement with the author

"Very little is needed to destroy a man;
he need only the conviction
that his work is useless."

Fyodor Dostoevsky

Prologue

The call came early in the morning from my sister Miriam. "Hullo," I answered dully, not fully awake.

"Al, it's Mim. Are you up?"

I licked my dry lips and sat up creaking. I blinked a few times trying to focus. "Yeah, Mim. I'm up. Not functioning yet, but up. What's the matter?"

Even over the phone, I could hear her take a deep breath, "It's Pop. He's gone. He died a couple of hours ago. The hospital called me, but I had my phone turned off until just now."

I could hear her sniffling. She was speaking in a rush, trying to get it all out without me interrupting,

"As soon as I turned my phone back on, there was a message. He died during the night. Oh, God, I should have been with him, but, Al, I've been there so much these last couple of weeks, and I just came home to try to get in a few hours sleep before going back. Oh, please don't hate me, Al; I've been with him so much. Can you meet me here? Please come, Al. I need you here to help me. You know Sammy is no help and I …"

I broke in as soon as I understood what she was trying to say. My father had died last night. Old Herschel Rothberg had kicked the bucket. "Take it easy, Mim. It's all over now. Let me grab a shower and

I'll meet you at the hospital in an hour. I'll call Sammy. You don't have to."

"Thanks, Al," she whispered. "Thank you, thank you, thank you. Please hurry, and could you bring me a coffee? I don't think I can stop. I don't think I can face anybody right now."

"Yeah, sure, Mim. I'll be there. Drive carefully." I hung up. Son-of-a-bitch, so the old man finally cashed in his chips. Hell of a life, I thought. He and my Uncle Hans, what a couple of guys. Almost like a married couple.

My wife rolled over and without opening her eyes, she muttered, "Who was that, Al?"

"Nothing, Hon. Go back to sleep. I'll tell you later." And she did. My wife, Syl, was a doctor and didn't get in until late most nights. It had become a minor sore spot with us over the last few months since she'd been transferred to the ER.

I showered and dressed before calling my brother Sammy. He lived in LasVegas, but he'd been here a month ago when the old man had taken a turn for the worse. He'd lasted a week and couldn't stay. His job, he said. Some job, a dealer in Vegas. What kind of a job was that for a Jewish boy from Philly? With a sigh, I dialed his cell phone.

"Sam here, Al. What's up? Talk fast, I'm in the middle of a shift."

"Hey, Sammy. Just wanted to let you know that Pop passed away last night. We'll schedule the funeral for a couple of days. Call me back when you get a chance."

"No shit," he said slowly, letting out a breath. "I'll call you as soon as I get off. Love to Mim."

The phone went dead in my ear. I shrugged. Sammy and the old man never did get along and he was gone the minute he'd graduated from high school, hitchhiking to California and becoming a surf bum. That had developed into a job making boards, then film school and he made a couple of documentaries. One was about surfing in Mexico, and the next one was about sailing, I think. I kind of lost track of him for a few years. I'd heard through Mim that he'd been married, divorced, had a couple of kids, sold insurance, and had and lost a few other jobs.

I kissed my wife's forehead and walked out to my car, which was parked in the driveway. The sun was just coming up. It was going to be another sunny and dry day here in Philly. I stopped at the nearest Starbucks and picked up coffees for Mim and me.

Her car was in the visitors' lot at Beth Israel when I got there, though parked crooked, like she'd been in a hurry. Why she was rushing to see a dead man in a depressing hospital was beyond me. The place was just a pile of bricks dating from just after the war, though I really didn't know which one. The paint was peeling over the doors and the floor tiles were a dull green. As I walked in, a barely coherent message was sounding over the squawk box. The doctors and nurses must have figured out the language code being used. I sure couldn't.

Mim was sitting on a couch in the lobby. I just handed her the coffee and sat beside her, our thighs touching. She was in a dark pantsuit and a white blouse with a skinny piece of ribbon tied droopily at her throat. Her eyes looked dark and she'd only run a brush a couple of times through her cap of black hair. I noticed a couple of gray hairs at her temples. It jolted me. I always considered her to be 'the kid'. Sammy was the youngest but Mim was my kid sister and had always acted like one. I knew she was in her forties, but Mim with gray hair? Wow! She had been a high school teacher and had just the one kid, Joanie, now away at Berkeley. She and her abusive husband, French, had divorced a few years ago and, last I heard, French was doing hard time for screwing a bunch of retirees out of their life savings in some kind of Ponzi scheme. I wondered if Ponzi knew how famous he would become?

"You O.K., kid?" I asked putting my arm around her.

She nodded, tears running down her cheeks. "I couldn't go in to look at him alone, Al." She pulled out a crumpled tissue and wiped ineffectually at her eyes. "I'm glad you're here."

I sipped my coffee, "C'mon. Let's get it over with." I helped her to her feet and we took the elevator to the third floor. A nurse was just coming out of Pop's room and held the door for us. I'd met her on several of my trips here and said, "Thanks, Doris."

"I'm so sorry, Al, Miriam. I wasn't on duty but Sheila said she was with him and he died quietly and didn't suffer."

We thanked her and went inside. The curtain was pulled around his bed. The other bed, the one closest to the door, was empty and had been for a few days. Nobody dying to get it, I thought. I went through the curtain, holding it aside for Mim. She went over to the opposite side of the bed and took a deep breath, steeling herself. After her husband left, she and Pop had gotten close. Little Joanie had spent a lot of time with the old man, telling each other lots of stories, some of them even true, no doubt.

She nodded and I pulled the sheet back. Pop's face was pale; his hair sparse and neatly combed. I expect Doris or Sheila had fixed him up. He had a faint smile on his clean-shaven face. It was a strong face, square chin and a large hooked nose with close-set eyes. He looked like a cross between a human and an eagle. His lipless mouth just turned up at the corners. I always kidded him that he had Meg Ryan's mouth. He still did. Mim was crying again, her shoulders shaking, her arms crossed in front of her chest.

I went around and held her tight, and she soaked my shirt. At last she stopped. I was about to pull the sheet back up when she stopped me. "Goodbye, Poppa. I love you." She stooped and kissed him on the forehead, then turned and walked out.

I looked at the tranquil face. "Hell of a life, Pop. I loved you, too." And I kissed him on the forehead beside Mim's kiss.

After that, things became quite a blur of death certificates, funeral arrangements, canceling his credit cards, phone service, email accounts, and paying all the final bills. I took care of all this and the next day, picked Sammy up from the airport. Mim wasn't much help, although she made the arrangements for the caterer after the memorial service to be held two days later.

Sammy helped her and the turnout was larger than expected. Pop had had a lot of friends and a lot of Uncle Hans' friends showed up too. The big house was filled with people eating, drinking and talking. As I made the rounds, I kept hearing folks telling stories about the Gruesome Twosome, as they called my Pop and his brother.

Pop's lawyer, Saul Goldman, was there and he pulled me aside, "Ancel, come and see me in a couple of days." He looked at the calendar on his watch, "Say, Thursday around three and we'll go over the will, O.K.?"

I nodded. Nobody but Saul ever called me by my given name. When I was growing up, our neighborhood had been heavily Italian and a kid with a name like Ancel would have been beaten up a lot. So I shortened it to Al. My Social Security card even listed me as Al. The Social Security lady wanted to know if it was Albert or Alfred or what, but I insisted, just Al and she finally gave in. It took my parents longer to accept the name change, but when I wouldn't answer to Ancel, they got used to it.

Thursday came, and Sammy and I picked up Mim to go to the lawyer's office. My brother was staying with Syl and me. We'd taken a couple of long walks, remembering Pop and Uncle Hans. We even went to the little park where they liked to sit on a bench and ogle the young mothers and nannies in the summer.

Saul's office was in a tall, imposing building down near Market Street in the heart of the financial district. It had beautifully gilded doors that were curved at the tops like doors in the old cathedrals. That always impressed me whenever I'd gone there with Pop. It was funny, Saul was normally a very respectable corporate lawyer. I could never figure out what caused him to accept Pop as a client. Pop and Uncle Hans just owned a hardware store, and it wasn't even incorporated, as far as I knew.

After we were shown into his office and seated, Saul's secretary brought us coffee. After the usual amenities were concluded, I asked, "Saul, you and Pop were friends for a long time but you were always a big shot, and Pop, well, Pop was always, for lack of a better word, a little shot."

"Yeah, Saul, what's up with that?" asked Sammy.

Saul just looked at us for a minute. Then he pulled back the sleeve of his expensive suit jacket and removed the heavy gold cufflink from his crisp broadcloth shirt. He shoved the sleeve back and turned his arm so we could see the faded blue tattooed number inside his forearm. "I was in Auschwitz. Your father and Uncle Hans were in the camps too. That's why."

Sammy and I nodded. Saul pulled his sleeve down, inserted the cufflink and replaced his coat sleeve. A bond like that can be stronger than family.

Saul cleared his throat and read the will. Pop's estate was to be divided equally among us, the house was to be sold and profits also divided among us. I was appointed executor, then Miriam, and then Sammy, in that order. Pop wasn't rich just very comfortable, but the amount of the bequest was more money than I'd expected. Then Saul handed me a thick manila envelope, almost an inch thick. "Herschel wanted you three to have this. You're supposed to read it together."

"What's it about, Saul?" Sammy asked.

Saul shrugged, "I don't know. Your father and Uncle Hans asked me not to read it, so I didn't." He sat back, and his chair creaked. Saul folded his thick hands across his ample belly. "Any questions?" He looked from one to the other of us. Nothing. Smiling, he said, "No? Then get the hell out of here and let me get some work done!"

We decided to go back to Mim's place. Joanie was at school, and the house was empty. I phoned my wife, told her what happened and that I'd be home later. She was at the hospital and couldn't talk. So what else was new?

Mim made coffee for the three of us and brought out a plate of homemade apple strudel cut into pieces. When we were all seated, I opened the envelope.

CHAPTER 1
Herschel and Hans

My Dear Children: Miriam, Ancel, and Sammy,

If you are reading this, I am dead. Dead, not 'passed away' or 'deceased'. Let's call it what it is. Your Uncle Hans is dead too, but we felt that there is something you ought to know. As they say on the television, things aren't always as they seem. I leave it to you if you should share this information with Hans' children, your cousins Ruthie and Nathan, though we felt that we'd leave it to you three, to decide if they should know too. My lawyer, Saul, has held this letter for many years. It's sealed so he doesn't know what's in it. This is a story, your Uncle Hans', and mine. I imagine you're going to get upset because this story is quite different from what we told you when you were growing up. If so, please forgive us. The truth? Well, you'll see for yourself.

First of all, your Uncle Hans is not really your uncle. What I mean is that he's not really my brother, though a better brother in this entire world I could never hope to have. I once had an older brother named Isaac. I also had a sister named Miriam. Yes, Miriam, you are named after her. I was the youngest child of three and we lived in a nice town in Eastern Germany called Teplice. My father and his father had been jewelers. The Nazis killed my family during the war. I saw my father and grandfather shot out front of our shop. My mother and sister were raped, and sent to the women's' extermination camp in Ravensbruck where I later learned they were gassed and burned. I'm telling you this in brutal terms so you will get a feeling for what we all went through.

I was separated from my brother and sent to the concentration camp at Kefferstadt. This was a sub-camp of Dachau. Being older, he went to a different camp. I never did find out what happened to him.

Did you know that the British General Herbert Kitchener, before he was awarded his Lordship, invented concentration camps during the Second Boer war? He rounded up guerilla fighters and civilians and concentrated them into large camps. Interesting, no?

Anyway, I met your Uncle Hans in the camp where I was a prisoner. At the time I was fifteen years old and he was sixteen. I'd been at the camp for almost three years before he showed up. This happened near the end of the war, as it turned out, only five months until the American army liberated us.

At the time, I was a Sonderkommando or Special Command Unit. These units were comprised of Jews whose job was to remove the corpses from the gas houses, transport them to the trenches and bury them. We also collected their possessions, pulled gold teeth and a sorted and catalogued the belongings. Yes, my job was as a Sonderkommando.

In the early days, when the camps were being set up, the people were told that they were going to shower. They were instructed to pile their clothes and possessions in bins we had made. The Nazi guards even went so far as to allow the men and women to be sent in separately. Later they stopped being so nice and we Sonderkommando had to strip both the men and the women of all their clothing. I had never even seen a woman naked. For years afterward I had terrible flashback images of all those naked women's bodies. I even had bad dreams when I saw your mother naked, as beautiful as she was.

Several of us younger and stronger fellows, loaded the corpses onto low-wheeled trolleys and took them to the trenches. After we dumped our fellow Jews, gypsies, homosexuals and 'enemies of the state' into the trenches, we ran back to the gas building and gathered up the piles of goods and took them to a central warehouse where we distributed them into the appropriate bins. We stole and hid what we could, which wasn't much because we were guarded closely, especially in the early days. In the evenings, before we were sent back to our barracks, the guards stripped us and inspected our clothes, often beating us with clubs and short whips for no reason. It got to be routine and I hated the guards who did this. Hated them with a passion that burns in me to this day. I still bear the scars on my back and in my joints from the brutality. Not all guards were so brutal though, and towards the end of the war, youngsters nearly my own age replaced the older guards. This lessened the number of beatings as the younger guards saw us as nearly like them. I sometimes slipped a gold tooth to one particular guard. He rarely hit me. I don't know if he shared with the other guards or with the commandant, a Major Boettcher. I suspect he didn't, but who can say? Those were terrible times and nothing really made any sense. We worked hard. The trains kept coming, bringing more and more people until I wondered if there was anyone left in Europe. Perhaps the young guards were frightened as the war's end approached.

But the trains grew fewer, perhaps due to increased Allied bombings, lack of fuel or a scarcity of enemies of the state. Soon they stopped altogether. Many of the other inmates died from diseases like malaria, tuberculosis, scurvy, or just wore out. As the guards, those still of fighting age, were rounded up and sent to the fronts, this left just a couple of old men, pensioners from the last war, as if there were any more pensions to collect; and finally, towards the end, some of the Hitler Youth lads. Most of these were too young to fight in regular army units, but they were the only ones left to guard the camps.

I hope you're sitting down when you read this. Your Uncle Hans was a member of the Hitler Youth (Hitler-Jugend or HJ) and a camp guard.

I know what you're thinking. How could that be? He was such a good Jew. He was my brother and your uncle. Yes, yes, that was what you were supposed to think. Wait, Hans wants to say something here.

* * *

Oy, your father simply runs on and on, doesn't he? Now for my story, if anyone is interested. You know all the old tales about how your father and I fought in the Warsaw Ghetto together, how we were in a camp and came to America after the war? O.K., so it's partly true, only not the part about the Warsaw Ghetto. We were in a camp and did come to America together.

Didn't you children once ask why we had no tattoos on our forearms? Do you remember what I said? That I was a latecomer and that there was no one to run the tattoo needle on the day I came to the camp? Well, your Pop and I weren't at Auschwitz, and that was the only camp that tattooed prisoners. But the real reason is because I wasn't a prisoner. I was a guard.

I was born and brought up in a town near the Black Forest close by the Austrian border. I had a normal childhood. I went to school, joined the Boy Scouts, had a sister named Ilsa and a father who was a middle manager at a nearby Daimler Benz factory. My mother was sickly and died when I was eight.

Ilsa and I were close, and it was she who introduced me to the Deutsches Jungvolk, the junior version of the Hitler Youth. I loved it. We went camping and I learned to shoot a gun and ride a horse. We sang songs and took part in rallies. By the time I was fourteen, I was head of my cell. I tried to enlist in the Waffen SS, but I was too young and my father, who was a good member of the party, wouldn't lie for me. Instead, I helped the local police. We watched for saboteurs and made sure that people used their blackout curtains. To my everlasting shame, I also helped round up Jews and vandalized their shops and homes. In other words, I was a good little Nazi boy.

We all knew the war was ending and not in a good way for the German people again. So I was surprised when I got a call from our district commander. He was an older man named Strichcher, who had lost an arm and one eye in the last war. He told me to pack a bag and take a train to Kefferstadt, a camp near Dachau. I was excited. I was going to war! I bade my father and sister goodbye, and went off the next day. Shortly after that, our town was bombed, and my father and sister were killed. I didn't find this out until much later.

And so I came to the camp known as Kefferstadt. It was a small, remote camp out in the country, almost five miles from the nearby town of Keffer. Along the front of the camp was a tall row of barbed wire stretching between two high guard towers, with a gate in the center. The barbed wire was nailed to posts set about two meters apart. In the rear was only one guard tower but it had a powerful searchlight and was always manned. Inside the gate was a long building. This contained Commandant Boettcher's office and quarters, the guard's barracks, and the mess hall. These buildings were made of wood, whitewashed with green trim, very neat, very German. In the compound were two stone buildings that looked like cottages and a row of six wooden buildings. These were the barracks for the prisoners. They were also made of wood, though not painted or trimmed. The roofs were corrugated tin and leaked when it rained, I learned later. Inside were rows of wooden shelving racks, three high, with no bedding. The men slept on the bare wood.

There were no provisions for women. They were gassed as soon as they arrived at the camp. I thank God I never had to witness this shameful deed. Off to the side was a smaller building that I learned was the kitchen for the prisoners. It was almost a lean to with one side open to the wind. They had no mess hall and ate their two - sometimes one meal - per day outdoors or, in the winter, in the barracks.

I was given a uniform that was too large and a rifle and told that we were to operate the camp as before and await orders. I met your father one day when we were both ordered to sort through the valuables in the storeroom. I assumed they were getting ready to ship these things to Berlin. At first I spoke harshly to him, after all, I was older and a good Nazi and he, a despised Jew.

CHAPTER 2
Herschel's Story

I have to tell you what my life was like, my beautiful children. Up until the time I was about eight, it was idyllic. We lived in town, in a big apartment behind the jewelry store. My father and grandfather would go out front each day and open the shop that had been in the family for years. My sister Miriam, my brother Isaac and I would go off to school. My mother would clean the house and make some jewelry designs for the shop. My Bubby had died while I was a baby. Miriam said she remembered her, but I think she was just referring to the picture that hung in our parlor.

The first time I remembered things not being good was a day when I was walking home from school and some boys started yelling at me. They hollered, "Jew, Jew!" and threw rocks at Isaac and me. We ran, Isaac pulling on my hand to make me run faster. When we got to the shop, my Papa, who was a big man, strode outside and shook his fist at the boys and yelled back at them.

After that day, it got worse. Over the next two years, we took a different route home from school each day until the groups of boys got larger. Soon they were waiting at all of our routes. Isaac sometimes got into fistfights, but there were too many of them. He was slight yet wiry, like my Mama, and full of fire. He beat them back lots of times, especially when he called them cowards and took them on one at a time. I tried to help him and though I was tall for my age, was slim and might have filled out like my Papa if I'd had the chance. At the time, however, I was too little to fight.

Then one night in 1938 a large group of men and boys, people we knew and had never had any problems with, came down our street in what was called the Jewish Quarter. They started throwing rocks through windows as they walked, chanting and yelling. By the time they got to our shop, they had worked themselves into an angry mob. What was even more disturbing is that they were joined by some policemen, men who were supposed to protect us.

Why were they angry with us? I spotted Mr. Bruger and his son Leny there. They were yelling very loudly and holding torches. Just two weeks before, Mr. Bruger had bought a pin for his wife's birthday from Papa. My brother and Leny were in the same classes. When Papa and Grandpapa came out front and stood before the door, they each had long sticks in their hands.

Papa tried to talk to them, saying that whatever they were angry at, it wasn't anything he had done. He pointed to Mr. Bruger and Mr. Schmidt and Mr. Westergarten and asked what they wanted. I stood in the doorway with Isaac. Mama and Miriam stood way back in the dark shop, keeping very quiet. Papa and Grandpapa had told them to do so.

Mr. Bruger yelled, “You are Jews!”

“Yes,” my Papa answered. “You’ve known that all our lives. Why does that make a difference now?” He stood erect, tapping the stout stick against his boot. My Grandpapa leaned on his, hat pulled low on his face. I thought he looked like one of those cowboys in the American movies.

In answer, Mr. Bruger threw a stone that hit my father in the chest and bounced off. To his credit, Mr. Bruger, a slim and balding fellow, looked sheepish. Then a policeman drew his pistol and shot the large front window out. It shattered into millions of pieces. Most fell inward, while some large pieces dropped and exploded into the street. Everyone was quiet for a minute not knowing what to do next.

Papa strode up to the policeman and, towering over him, asked in a loud voice, “What the hell did you do that for? You’ll pay for that glass.”

Then, to the astonishment of all, the policeman shot my father point blank into his chest. Papa stared at the hole in his shirt, the red spreading. Then he looked up and hit the policeman with his stick so hard that the side of the policeman’s face just crumpled. He fell at my Papa’s feet and then Papa fell to his knees, one hand over his chest and finally collapsed on top of the policeman.

My grandpapa ran to my father and another policeman shot him in the head. He, too, fell forward. My mother and Miriam screamed and ran out of the shop, pushing past Isaac and me. I wanted to run too, but Isaac’s grip on my shoulder was like an iron vise.

Before Mama and Miriam could get to Papa and Grandpapa, the crowd grabbed them and tore their clothes from their bodies. I turned my face into Isaac's chest and cried. I was ten years old, and I cried like a little baby. Later Isaac, who was thirteen, told me that the men, our former friends and neighbors, had raped them repeatedly. Then they rushed into the shop. Isaac and I were dragged out and punched and kicked until we lost consciousness.

When we awoke, it was dawn. The street was clear of men, and the sun glinted on a carpet of shards of glass. I read later that this was called "Krystall Nacht" because of all the glass. We never saw Mama or Miriam again. We heard that they had been sent to a work camp called Ravensbrueck, but it turned out to be an extermination camp for women. I only knew of my Mama's and sister's fate from a ledger that was recovered by the Russians from the partially demolished camp. Years later they gave a copy to the British, who published the list. Until then, I never knew, and it haunted me.

Isaac and I hid in our apartment behind the shop and survived, often scuttling through the streets and alleys late at night and searching through garbage cans for food, like the rats they called us.

One night Isaac spotted Mr. Bruger, and we followed him. He had been one of the men who had cheered when my papa and grandpapa had been shot. He'd been one of the men who had torn the clothes from my mother and sister and held them while the men had raped and raped them. He had once been a friend, we thought. Isaac was crazed that night. When Mr. Bruger was opposite an alley entryway, Isaac grabbed him and pulled him in. After a brief struggle, Isaac hit

Mr. Bruger on the head with a cobblestone. He hit him and hit him until there was nothing left of his pinched face.

After that we were hunted and finally we were caught. Isaac tried to stay with me, but he was sent to a camp called Gross-Rosen, in the east of Germany. I was sent to a small camp named Kefferstadt near the Swiss border. It was a sub-camp of the much larger one at Dachau, though I was never there, thanks be to God. You could smell the stench from Dachau all the way to our camp in the woods some days. There were never more than four or five hundred of us in Kefferstadt. I was now thirteen and almost two meters tall, though very thin.

The Nazis usually sent boys younger than fifteen off to be gassed but I lied and was tall so they let me live. Can you call what I did living?

Sonderkommando is what we were called. I, and a few others, would go into the gas buildings after everyone was dead and the gas had dissipated, pull the bodies out, and transport them to the trenches dug between the back fence and the wood. The clothing, valuables, shoes and even the underclothes were all taken to the counting shed. We separated the valuables and once a week a courier from Berlin would come and retrieve the best items. They weren't interested in the clothing, so the counting house, began to fill up though mice and moths enjoyed the feasts there.

I think Kefferstadt was originally designed as a work camp. One of the older prisoners told me that early in the war there were sewing machines and they made uniform blouses for SS officers. All that was now forgotten, and that building sat unused.

We were merely a disposal camp. I'm sure that the Commandant at Dachau, who was the OberKommandant of the main camp and the dozens of sub-camps, had forgotten us. Our Major Boettcher supposedly reported to him.

CHAPTER 3
HANS' Story

I came to Kefferstadt on a cool, overcast day. I got off the train in the nearby town of Keffer, but there was no one at the station to meet me. I waited for more than an hour but still no one came. Finally I asked the stationmaster how I could get to Kefferstadt. He told me that it was down a road to the east. It was early autumn, and the weather was still warm. When the wind let up a bit and the sun came out, I started walking, my bag perched on my shoulder. As I walked, the fields gave way to a small forest. It was beautiful, with the leaves turning color, all golden and red. One would not know there was a war on.

After a while, a farm cart pulled by a skinny nag came along and the driver let me ride with him. He was thin and bent, wisps of gray hair peeking out from under a battered straw hat. When I told him my destination, he shook his head and muttered something I didn't quite understand, something about an abattoir and hell.

At last we came to a fork in the road and he pointed to the left. About one-half kilometer, he said, and threw my bag down. By the time I alighted and had retrieved my bag, all I saw was the back of the cart. Then he was gone around a sharp bend.

I came to the gate in the late afternoon. There was one guard. When I showed him my papers, he let me in and directed me to the Commandant's office. My first impression of the camp was gray. Everything was gray, nothing painted. A row of ramshackle barracks obviously for the prisoners, weathered wood with rusty corrugated metal roofing. Rows of barbed wire surrounded the camp. As I entered through the gate, to my left was the Commandant's Office. Like the rest, it was a wooden framed building with corrugated iron roofing, similar to the prisoners' barracks, though somewhat better constructed. At one time it may have been painted but that was long ago and only a few flakes remained. There was a narrow porch but no chairs or tables on it. It was merely meant to provide a place to stand in inclement weather while waiting for the commandant's secretary to allow admittance.

A Major Boettcher was Commandant and took my papers. My first impression of him was that he was a professional soldier, in his fifties with a square jaw, close-cropped graying hair and a short fleshy nose. What I most remembered was his eyebrows. Thick and dark, almost obscuring his pale gray eyes. He snorted, "Kinder, all I get is kinder." He turned to me with a sigh, "Go to your barracks and draw a uniform and weapon. It is the second building on the left as you exit. If you can't find it, Schwartz or one of the other guards will show you." I left him looking down at a newspaper, head in hands.

I found the barracks and a sergeant named Granski. I introduced myself and offered him my hand.

He snorted and slapped it away, "So you are here to help exterminate the rats, eh?" He was squat with greasy black hair and bristly black whiskers.

I was confused. Rats? Were we overrun with rats? I looked around at the dingy barracks room. It was dark, and the place was long overdue for paint. Three dim light bulbs glowed trying to seep into the gloom between bunk beds and lockers. The windows were coated with grime and the floor with dirt and dust. So this was my new home.

I frowned at Sgt. Granski. "Rats?"

He chuckled, "Rats. Jews. Queers. They are all the same. We keep them here until the Reich tells us to grind up another batch." He grinned through widely gapped teeth. Then he turned on his heel and led me to a bunk with a half folded mattress. It was thin and smelled of mold.

I looked at the rows of bunk beds. "How many guards are there, Sergeant? There must be a large contingent to fill this room."

"Only ten now, young Hans. But now we only have about one-hundred and fifty rats to guard." He laughed again and snorted, "Guard! As if any of the rats are going anywhere. They couldn't even if they wanted to."

I frowned, "Why is that, Sergeant?"

He grinned. "Too weak. Too sick. Too scared."

And so that was my introduction to the camp at Kefferstadt and one of my fellow guards. We kept the gate closed and sat in the towers or fed the guard dogs. The camp kept several large Alsatians. I was told that at one time, this camp bred the guard dogs.

Sometimes a truck would bring a couple of new prisoners but even that finally ceased. Once I saw a guard shoot a prisoner for no apparent reason, out of boredom I expect. I was not much given to abusing the rats, as the prisoners were called, though if one were slow, I was ordered to give him a rough shove.

Food was our biggest problem. The nearby farmers had stopped coming around and after our petrol got low, we were unable to go get food in the town. We grew a small garden and some of us hunted the surrounding wood. One day a farmer came with a cart with cabbages in it. We offered him Reichmarks but he refused, preferring gold or gems.

That was just about the time I met your father personally. One day I was told to help out in the storage warehouse. There was a rat there that knew gold and gems.

"What do you know of these valuables, Jew?" I asked, shoving him but not too roughly. The boy was thin as a rail, though tall, with brown hair and a small, bent nose, unlike the Jews shown on the posters pasted up in my hometown. The more I looked at the boy, the more curious I became. Take away the striped uniform and he looked like one of the boys I'd been with in school or the Hitler Youth. "Where are you from, boy?"

Herschel looked up and frowned, then dropped his eyes, "I am from a town in Eastern Germany near Dresden, Teplice. My family are, or," he mumbled, "were jewelers."

"Jewelers, huh? So what do you know about this stuff, Jew? Or should I call you Jew-eler?" I said in jest. I picked up some of the pins, necklaces, rings and bracelets, then let them slide through my fingers into a wooden tray.

He slid down onto the floor and held the tray in his lap. "Come, sir, sit down here and I will teach you about gold and what I know of gems." He looked at me appraisingly, "My name is Herschel. What is yours, sir?"

I sat down beside him after leaning my heavy rifle against the wall. "I am Hans, Herschel," and shook his thin hand. And from that day on I was the student of a rat - or the first Jew I had ever known.

Later we became friends. Ironic, no? He would help me select some semiprecious gem or gold trinket to trade for food. We eventually made a small cache of the better items and buried them in a jar I'd taken from the kitchen.

It seemed like each day we would have to bury a prisoner or two. By the time I had arrived, very few prisoners were shipped to us. The ones we had were sick and weak. After only one month, our population had dwindled to little more than one hundred prisoners and only seven guards. With the lack of food and petrol, we guards were in no better physical condition than the prisoners. So why did we stay? Why did we not leave as two guards did one day, just laying down their rifles and walking out the gate? I suppose that some of us felt it was our duty to stay and yet, with the war all but over, we knew that we would be punished as harshly as any of the prisoners, maybe even worse. I stayed because I had no one to go home to. No home, in fact. My school friends were scattered, father and sister dead. One day I realized that my only friend was Herschel. I treated him as an equal and brought him scraps of food. I tried to protect him from the abuses of the other guards. Granski was the worst. He said he enjoyed killing the rats, that he was doing the world a favor. I grew up quickly in this camp. Many times the farmer's words came back to me: abattoir, hell.

I wore shoes taken from the storehouse, a baggy pair of trousers, which barely reached to my calves and my uniform coat and hat. I had neither undergarment nor socks, for these had all fallen apart many weeks ago, and there were none to be had in the storehouse. Herschel gave what clothes he could to the other prisoners, and I assisted him. Our storehouse seemed to be the dispensary, clothing store, cooking utensil supply and shroud source.

Oh, yes, we had lots of shrouds. In the beginning we received many hundreds of burial shrouds. Now we were tearing them up for rags and dressings for the many weeping sores. Yes, I lived with my friend in hell.

CHAPTER 4
Herschel's Story

Hans became my pupil. Most days we prisoners were roused from our pallets with a kick and were shoved ahead of guards to tables and benches for some food, though food was a polite term. These days every meal was a thin, watery gruel. Sometimes there were maize granules, pig feed; or small pieces of root vegetables, rarely meat. Two of the guards trekked into town and traded gold teeth or small pins for whatever they could find. Sometimes they would commandeer a cart and horse from a farmer to bring them back.

A guard named Jurgen was the cook for both the guards and the prisoners. The war was nearing the end, and we were all starving, guards and prisoners alike. The prisoners wore striped uniforms, though rags were more like it, while the guard's uniforms had deteriorated to a like state. There were few clothes remaining in the counting house and what was there were mainly children's and women's. The moths and rats had made Swiss cheese of most of them.

One day, as we crouched in the sorting house, we were discussing the carat weight of gold. For some reason, Hans asked me what my family name was. Now, he had rarely talked about family, his or mine. "Why do you ask, Hans?" I warily questioned. Was he trying to get some information from me?

He shrugged, "Just want to know who I am working with."

I was taken aback. Working with? Not 'had under me' or 'who my prisoner is', but *working with*. I was almost loath to reply, but something compelled me to answer honestly. Hans had never abused me, never hit me. In fact he frequently gave me a crust of bread or an apple piece from his own larder.

I drew in a breath and said, "My full name is Herschel David Rothberg."

He jumped up, dropping the gold chain he'd been fingering, "You've gone too far, Jew. You make jest of me."

I frowned, frightened, "Why? What do you mean, Hans, I mean, sir?" I covered my head with my hands and leaned against the wall, drawing up my feet in expectation of a rain of blows.

He leaned forward, face almost touching mine. "My family name is also Rothberg, Herschel. How did you know? I never told you." He was angry and perplexed. He drew away and walked in close circles, muttering to himself.

I gaped, at him. "This is true? Rothberg? You are a Rothberg?" I couldn't help myself. I started laughing. What a cruel joke. I, a Jewish prisoner in a concentration camp, a death camp, shared the same family name with my guard, a good German boy, a Hitler Youth. I laughed. Lord, how I laughed, holding my sides, tears running down my face.

Hans understood the irony of it, and then he smiled. In a moment he started laughing too. Harder and harder. Oh, the paradox, that fate should give us this moment. Guard and prisoner shook with laughter, looking at each other and shaking with fresh gales.

I gasped, "Maybe we are long-lost brothers?" I shouted and collapsed again in mirth. I had not laughed in many years, and it felt so incredibly good. If I were to die at that moment, I would still have my laughter to transport me to who knows where.

After we had subsided, we two sat side by side against the wall. I was a bit taller than Hans. He was shorter but not quite as thin. His uniform trousers, worn through at the knees, were barely long enough to cover his ankles. I wore a pair of raggedy striped pants and a shirt that had once been a guard's waistcoat; shoes for both of us came from gassed and dead prisoners.

After a minute Hans asked me, "Where are your people from? Before coming to Germany, I mean."

I shrugged, "Someplace in Russia, my Grandpapa told us. I don't remember where. And yours?"

Now he shrugged, "Here. I mean Germany, as far as I know. Our family name many generations ago was Rothenberg, but somehow it got shortened to Rothberg." We both mulled that over.

Then, in a note of seriousness, he told me that the Commandant had left in the middle of the night in his auto, using the last of the petrol. Hans called the Commandant a coward and said, "There are only seven guards left to guard the prisoners." He buried his face in a crooked elbow "I don't know what will become of us."

"Why, what do you mean?" I asked.

"Granski, the Polish guard, now fancies himself Commandant. He wants us to kill all of the prisoners and run away so no one can tell what we did here. He sniffled and said, "But I have nowhere to go. My family was killed in an air raid. There are barely one-hundred of you prisoners left but I cannot let him kill all of you." He turned a haggard face to me, "What am I to do, Herschel? I have never killed anyone." His agony was plain to see.

I gasped, "You can't let him do that, Hans. These men are walking dead now." Most of the prisoners had been in the camp for years. The ones who are left have rheumatism, severe arthritis, tuberculosis, scurvy or a myriad of other ailments and diseases. I weighed just fifty kilos. We discussed ways to protect the other prisoners. Finally I demanded, "Who of the other guards are left?"

In an strained voice Hans replied, "Just me; Jurgen the cook; Helmut; Karl, the boy who came just last week from Hamburg; Riger; and, of course, Granski."

I thought for a moment, "Listen, Hans, this is what you must do." I grabbed him by a sleeve and thrust my face close. "Go into town tonight." I whispered. " Then when you get back, tell Granski that the British or Americans have parachuted into the forest near town and will be here by morning. That may make him leave during the night."

"But then what will we do, Herschel?" Hans was near tears.

Shrugging, defeated, I put my arm around the older boy and pulled him close and whispered, "We will wait.

The war will end soon, no? The Allies are nearby. The planes pass every night and the bombs are close to us. It can't be long now." I scrambled to my feet, pulling Hans up. "Now take me back to the barracks and go to town quickly." I knew I was taking a chance giving a guard orders, but by this time, Hans and I were more comrades than guard and prisoner; Hans and Herschel Rothberg.

CHAPTER 5

Hans' Story

I had come to this remote camp as a young boy. I had been protected by family and had belonged to a group of fellow boys much like the Boy Scouts; the Hitler Youth. I enjoyed my time with the other fellows, even when we were ordered to beat and round up Jews. I was told that the Jews were stupid, a sub-human species. They were also depicted as clever, money manipulators and, we were told they made items of gold and jewels stolen from our good German people. I had some trouble believing the claim that Jews were stupid; yet clever, and that they controlled all of the banking in the Reich. How could that be?

We took the Jews we arrested to a holding pen near the railroad yard in my town. I was told that this was happening all over Germany, and once all the Jews, Gypsies, homosexuals – I didn't know what this meant until later – and 'enemies of the state' were rounded up and sent to work camps, Germany would reclaim her rightful place as the leader of nations in the world.

My Papa used to tell me how bad things were after the Great War, a war we lost and then were treated very poorly by the Allies. It was Der Fuehrer who made us see how great we could be again. I was proud to be part of our recovery.

When I arrived at the camp, I was appalled. This was not a large camp, just six rough wooden buildings for the prisoners, and three somewhat smaller ones to the left of the gate for the guards and German support personnel. A cookhouse and kitchen for the guards and Commandant was next. Directly beside the gate was the main administrative office where the Commandant, Major Boettcher, his aide Sergeant Mueller, and a secretary worked.

The camp was surrounded by high barbed wire strands and had tall watchtowers in two of the corners. The camp was designed to hold almost one thousand prisoners, though I couldn't see where we could feed this many or even house them. I was disgusted at the condition of the prisoners. How could we keep these men working if they were in such poor physical condition? It took me only a couple of days to see that this was maybe once thought of as a work camp but was now an extermination camp. I was sickened and did everything I could to stay away from the gashouse. But one day I was ordered to help supervise the removal of bodies from this place.

That was when I met Herschel. He was about my age but taller. He moved swiftly and did the jobs assigned to him without lagging. I had no need to strike him or abuse him in any way. However, some of the other guards abused the prisoners whenever they could,

I think because they were bored. After a while, I saw him, not as a rat, but as a boy near my own age. He and I might have been friends back in my town.

He did not have the look of the stereotypical Jew: curly black hair, hooked nose, grasping hands that were on all the propaganda posters. He instead, had dark brown hair, green eyes, but with pale skin. His features were regular, and he often smiled. In our later discussions, I found him intelligent, respectful, quick, and most astonishing of all, not beaten down as most of the other prisoners seemed to be.

After a time, I tried to insert myself between the other guards and Herschel. I escorted him to the storehouse where the dead prisoners' belongings were sorted and kept until they could be sent to Berlin. Sometimes I was able to give him some food from the guard's kitchen.

As the war ground on, the trains grew fewer, then stopped. The prisoners ceased coming, and the belongings remained in the storehouse. No vehicles came to claim them. No further orders came from Berlin or Dachau. What is more, the supply trucks with our food stopped coming.

That is when Herschel started instructing me in the lore of precious metals and gems. I was an apt pupil, not long out of school, and the thirst for knowledge was still strong in me. Daily, I roused him with a light kick or a shove from his pallet in Barracks 4 and escorted him to his place in the kitchen area so he and I could eat what little food was available. Then we were off to the storehouse for the day's instruction. Sometimes one of the other young guards and I would go into the nearest town with a small bauble Herschel would select, and trade it for food or petrol, when there was some available.

I was worried that Granski, the older Polish guard, would kill all of the prisoners and possibly the rest of the guards. Several times he said, "If the Allies find out what has been done here, they will kill us all." He was referring to us guards and support personnel.

At Herschel's suggestion, he and I worked out a plan. I took some gold teeth and started walking to town. Security was now lax, with the few remaining guards in almost as poor condition as the prisoners. I was very weak, so I sat by the side of the road and fell asleep. I really did not have to go into Keffer to complete the ruse. I knew there was no food in the town.

I awoke in total darkness, disoriented and groggy. What woke me? Bombers overhead roared and dropped their bombs in the distance. I waited until they turned back and then hurriedly returned to the camp. Each time I left, I found it more and more difficult to return, but now I had Herschel as my friend, and I couldn't leave him to Granski.

Everything worked as we had planned. Well, almost. I rushed into the guard barracks and found Granski seated at a table eating the last of a piece of cheese. The other boys were asleep.

I whispered, "I heard that an American paratroop unit has landed on the other side of the town and might be upon us by morning." He jumped up and ran to our small larder, threw food into a cloth bag and grabbing a pistol, which he tucked into his belt. I followed him to the prisoner's kitchen, which he ransacked for what little food he could find.

A tall, gaunt prisoner who helped Jurgen, our cook, came in and asked, "What is happening?"

Soon two more prisoners crowded in, and the three made a feeble attempt to stop him. Granski drew the Luger pistol and shot them. Bang, bang, bang and the three fell dead at my feet, their blood pooling around and under them. At the noise, Herschel came in and stopped short. Granski turned the pistol on him, and I could see his finger tighten.

"Don't try to stop me, Jew," he spit.

Before he could shoot, I stepped between them. "Take what you want, Sergeant. No one will stop you," I said in as calm a voice as I could.

Granski jammed the pistol back into his belt and ran out without another word. We hoped to never see him again. I couldn't have stopped him nor would I. Granski ran through the open gate and disappeared down the road, the bag bouncing against his rounded back.

After that, we just waited, waited for the end and whatever that would bring. We foraged in the nearby wood and ate whatever we could catch or dig up. It seemed that the world had forgotten us, which was just as well.

CHAPTER 6
Herschel's Story

When I heard the gunshots, I ran from my pallet in Barracks 4. Hans was standing over three bodies, looking down in horror. Granski stood with his back against the wall, waving a Luger pistol and looking wild-eyed "They were going to attack me," he screamed. Then he aimed the pistol at me.

Just before Granski pulled the trigger, Hans stepped between us and said something to Granski. My heart stopped and I stood still, not daring to move. I looked down at Dovee, Mr. VanGelt and Professor Steiner lying in pools of blood, and then looked up at the pistol. I don't remember what Hans said, but Granski stuck the pistol in his belt and ran out. I couldn't move.

"Herschel, are you all right?" Hans shook me by the shoulder.

The tears ran down my face. I looked at him, "You saved my life, Hans." I looked down again at my friends and sighed. By now several more of the prisoners were gathered in the doorway to our little kitchen. "Please help me bury these good men." I went out to get my cart, and we placed the bodies on it, taking them to the mass grave at the back of the camp. Hans pointed a hand torch before us.

Rabbi Shmuel said a short prayer and we carried them down into the trench and laid them out. I shoveled enough dirt to cover them for the time being and climbed up, Hans helping me. We walked back to the barracks slowly, not talking. I bid him a good night and tried to sleep. At my count, we were down now to ninety-seven prisoners and only seven guards.

The next day was overcast, low dark clouds hanging over the camp. How appropriate, I thought. When we gathered for morning count, only Hans and two other guards emerged. I saw movement in the guards' barracks, but none of the others came to the muster. I'm not sure why we bothered every morning; force of habit, I guess. After the muster, most of the prisoners just sat against the walls of the buildings. Some went to the kitchen, and I walked toward the counting shed.

I watched Rabbi Shmuel take a pan of water in shaking hands to the dog kennel. We used to have five large and aggressive Alsatians, the breed you call German Shepherds. There were only two skinny dogs left now and no food. As if we would use what little food we had to feed the dogs.

We wanted to kill the dogs and eat them, but the Rabbi asked us to please not kill his kinder. There wasn't much meat on them anyway. He placed the bowl down on the ground and sat with the dogs. They looked longingly at him, hoping for some food, but all he had was a small brush, which he slowly stroked over their filthy coats. We were all prisoners.

Hans urged me to the storehouse, and we entered, and then sat on a rough bench against the wall.

I turned to my friend and again said, “You saved my life, Hans. I will never forget that.” I was an empty shell. I had come close to being exterminated so many times, but for some reason, the events of the past night loomed large in my mind. I was a prisoner in a concentration camp, and a guard had saved my life. Unheard of. We continued our jewelry lessons. It seemed pointless, but it passed the time.

By mid afternoon, my stomach was groaning. I was so hungry, I ached. Suddenly we heard a shot, then another. We lurched toward the door and stumbled outside. A light rain was falling, and the prisoners were gathered by the fence on the south side. Two guards squatted over an object. I hoped it wasn’t another one of my fellows.

Hans and I rushed through the gate and over to them. They were looking at a pig. It must have wandered out of the forest. Hans said to the men, “Why don’t you bring the pig to the cook house, and we will butcher it.” He sounded plaintive. A trickle of saliva ran down his chin.

I felt my own mouth moisten. A whole pig. Of course I knew pork was verboten to Orthodox Jews but I was so hungry. We hefted the carcass and carried it to the kitchen. It looked like it might weigh perhaps fifty kilos. One of the guards, Karl, I think, ran and got a length of rope. In short order the guards hoisted the dead pig up by a pulley hooked to a corner of the building’s roof. Everyone gathered round. Rabbi Shmuel said a short prayer and nodded. Two of the guards, both former farm boys, butchered the pig and cut it up into small pieces.

One of the prisoners, a man named David, edged forward and grabbed a small piece of flesh. The Rabbi struck his hand and knocked it to the ground. "You know why pork is forbidden. If we must eat it, it must be cooked through. He raised his eyebrows to the guards. They nodded.

Jurgen went to the kitchen storeroom and returned with a large kettle. While the guards threw in every edible piece of the pig, two prisoners brought buckets of water and poured them into the pot. Soon it was bubbling over a wood fire we'd built between several rocks.

More water was added, and a guard and a prisoner went into the nearby wood and returned with a mound of white roots. They, too, went into the pot along with the last of the salt. In an hour, everyone was lined up with his tin cup.

Even the guards took their place in line with their utensils. We were all in the same boat now.

My children, I have eaten many wonderful meals since that day, but no food ever tasted as sweet as that thin, watery stew. And pork, no less. I had never tasted pork. It was wonderful. Everyone had a cupful and though most wolfed it down, some, like Hans and I, savored every mouthful, trying to make it last. We had intended on saving some for another meal, but we were so hungry that before we knew it, the pot was empty.

Ah well, I felt human again. Hans and I and another guard, Helmut, sat on a bench against one wall of the administrative building.

"We need food, Hans. We need a regular supply. How can we get food?" There was no answer from either of them. We watched idly as Rabbi Shmuel patted the dogs and, with a smile for each of them, gently slumped to one side. One of the dogs whined and laid his head on the old man's lap. The other one just lay down next to the rabbi, nose under his hand. I nudged Hans and pointed.

Hans nodded. We stood and walked through the dust to the kennel. I leaned down and felt the old man's neck for a pulse. Nothing. He was dead. Just another old Jew dead in a Nazi camp. When I looked up, most of the other prisoners were standing behind us. A murmur lay over us like a blanket. I bent and closed the old man's eyes.

Hans nudged the dog next to the rabbi. Again, nothing. The dogs had been the rabbi's responsibility for so long that they died with him.

We wrapped Rabbi Shmuel in an old blanket and carefully laid him in the mass grave with a dog on either side of him. I mumbled a few words; a few of the others said some words, and we all said the Kaddish, the Hebrew prayer for the dead. And that was the end. We were now ninety-six. I wondered if it would ever end. Perhaps when, one by one, we were all laid in that deep trench beside the kind old man.

CHAPTER 7
Hans' Story

So the days went by and no one came. We took turns going to the village to try to trade for food. Though the trek was long, if we got an early start, we would warm up. The winter had been mild with only small patches of snow remaining beneath the trees. The other guards and prisoners foraged in the wood. It was late in the year and there had been some harvesting on the nearby farms and we were able to trade jewelry and gold teeth for some cattle corn and oats. It was meager fare, but we survived. Once in a while a guard would shoot a rabbit or a rodent to add to the pot.

We were standing in line one day, stamping our feet to stay warm, when two soldiers came down the road and stopped at our gate, which was left open these days. No one was going anywhere.

We just stood and stared. It had been so long since anyone had come through our gate. No one knew what to do.

The taller soldier made a fist and held it over his head. I saw a red star on his helmet and wondered if he was a Russian. I hoped not.

Herschel nudged me with an elbow. "Go see who they are," he hissed.

I looked around for my rifle and found it leaning against the wall of the cookhouse. I picked it up and, though it held no ammunition, I put it on my shoulder and walked to the gate.

"Who are you gentlemen?" I asked in German. I held the rifle across my chest as I'd been taught, at the ready.

The shorter soldier said something in what I thought was English. I smiled in relief and lowered my weapon. Then he hit me in the stomach with the butt of his rifle and screamed at me. I fell to the ground holding myself while the other soldier tore my weapon away and threw it out the gate. Herschel and two of the other guards, Helmut and Karl, came running up. The soldier fired his rifle into the air and Helmut and Karl dropped their weapons in fright, holding their arms up high. Herschel knelt in the dust beside me.

"Hans, Hans, are you all right?" he asked, feeling for broken ribs.

I pushed his hands away and gasped, "Yes, I am all right. Why did they hit me?"

Herschel looked up and screamed at them to go away, to leave us alone. The shot must have alerted more soldiers, for suddenly many were coming out of the wood on each side of the road, rifles pointed at us. There were nearly as many of them as there were of us. Herschel helped me to my feet and said something to the shorter soldier, the one who had hit me. His voice was now softer, in control.

"Why did you hit him?" he said in halting, school English.

The soldier smiled and laughed and said something to the other soldier. I noted that their uniforms were dirty, and the sleeve of one's shirt was nearly torn off. He had stubble of a beard but he was smiling at Herschel.

In a few moments a tall man, whom I assumed was an officer, pushed his way through the men surrounding us. I looked over my shoulder and saw that none of our people had moved. They were still in line with their tin cups or cans, watching raptly. The officer spoke to Herschel who shook his head.

"Slowly, please. It has been many years and I speak only small English. You are English?" Herschel asked, puzzling over the words.

The officer looked at this thin, brown-haired boy, "American. Does anyone else here speak English?"

Herschel slowly shook his head, "I do not think so. American. Is the war over, Mein Herr?"

The officer smiled and pulled a cigar out of his breast pocket, bit the end off and spit it in the dust. Then he jammed it into the corner of his mouth and lit it with a shiny silver lighter, "Almost, son, almost." Then he said something with a sneer in his voice but the only word I could understand was Nazis. He turned to another soldier, this one with several stripes on his sleeve, and in a moment the other soldier had shouted something and the American soldiers fanned out across the compound. They first collected the rifles from us guards and from the guards' quarters, and then they rounded up the seven of us and took us to our barracks.

Herschel tried to intervene but didn't have the words. One soldier put an arm over his shoulder and led him to the kitchen area. Herschel shouted to me but I could not understand what he said. The American soldiers shoved us roughly into the barracks and made us sit on two of the bunks. They kept their rifles ready as if we were going to overpower them. What a joke. I noted that some of them seemed no older than we were.

Karl asked for some water, but either the soldiers didn't understand or didn't care. I tried speaking to one of the men, a young fellow who looked little older than myself, but he shook his head and sneered at me, saying something guttural. What was the matter with these men? Did not one of them speak German?

An hour passed and Helmut asked to use the latrine. When a soldier looked at him questioningly, he pointed toward his crotch and made motions with his hand. The guard nodded and pointed to a bucket in a corner that was used for cigarette butts back when there was anything to smoke. He looked at me and I shrugged, "It's either that or in your trousers, Helmut."

Helmut sheepishly went into the corner and pissed into the bucket, trying to be as quiet as possible. The soldiers snickered but kept their rifles at the ready.

About one hour later a small, dark haired man my father's age came in. He had thick glasses and a battered leather briefcase under his arm. His uniform was rumpled and, though his rank appeared to be a lieutenant, the soldiers deferred to him. The soldiers had moved our battered desk into the center of the room. He sat there, lit a cigarette and surveyed us.

I watched as he withdrew several items from the briefcase and placed them carefully on the desktop. Then he barked in German, "You!" and gestured at Karl. "Who is in charge here?"

Karl looked at each of us in turn. We all shrugged. No one had been, as they say, in charge, since Granski had left. Actually, no one had been in charge since the commandant had driven away one night many months ago. "Excuse me, sir, but no one is in charge. We've just stayed here."

He looked bewildered. No one in charge? Inconceivable. "Who is the senior man then?" he asked.

After some discussion amongst us, it was decided that Karl was the oldest, having turned eighteen just three weeks previously. We pointed at Karl.

I wondered what they were doing to Herschel and the other men.

CHAPTER 8
Herschel's Story

The soldier held me by my arm. I hollered over my shoulder to Hans, but the other soldiers pushed him and the other guards roughly into their barracks. I struggled to get free, but the soldier was much stronger than I. He must have thought I wanted to kill the guards. What was going to happen to us, all of us?

One of the prisoners stepped forward. I knew his name was Shlomo, but everyone called him Sy. I seemed to recall that he'd been a teacher or a professor at a university near Hamburg. He held his hands over his head, palms out and walked toward the soldiers. He was thin and wobbled on toothpick legs. What rags he wore hung on him like so much dirty laundry. His few teeth garbled his words at first but one of the soldiers came forward and listened to him. I could tell he didn't understand what Sy was saying, but he listened patiently, nodding. He pulled Sy's hands down, but Sy was afraid and kept raising them. The soldier gave up. He dropped the butt of his rifle next to his foot and a little puff of dust rose and then settled. For some reason I remember that little puff of dust. I think it marked the end, or maybe a new beginning.

The soldier reached into his pocket and pulled out what looked to us like a green stick and handed it to Sy. The soldier watched as Sy smelled it, threw his head back and laughed. Cackled was more like it. He tore the olive drab wrapper and broke a piece off, and popped it reverently into his mouth. A look of joy suffused his wrinkled face. He turned and shuffled back to the others who still stood in line waiting their turn for the corn meal mush. Tears ran down his weathered face as he broke off small pieces and handed them to those near him. There were only six or eight pieces, so I didn't get one, but the looks on the faces of those that did was absolutely amazing.

Sy whispered to himself, "It's chocolate." We who had been living on next to nothing for so long, we who had lost at least one third of our body weight, we who had been systematically starved and worked to near death by the Nazi guards had the first taste of food from outside in the form of a chocolate bar. It was transforming. It lit up faces that hadn't smiled in years.

Sy threw his arms up in the air and shouted loudly in German, "It is chocolate! These soldiers are Americans! We are saved!"

The crowd of men started to surge forward toward the soldiers who looked nervous, but held their ground. These soldiers who had fought their way across Europe and into the heartland of Nazi Germany looked frightened of a rag-tag band of walking scarecrows. Many years later I saw a movie called "Night of the

Living Dead". It was about zombies. The way they shuffled toward the camera, that is what the crowd of prisoners must have looked like to the soldiers.

The big officer stepped forward and held up a hand. My fellow prisoners stopped. The officer said out of the corner of his mouth, "Come here, kid."

The soldier gently pushed me toward him, and I stumbled. "What do you wish, sir?"

"Listen carefully, kid." He leaned toward me and put a huge hand on my shoulder, "Tell them to relax. In a little while a couple of trucks will show up with food. We'll feed them all and get them into some decent clothes. You understand me?"

I didn't understand all the words, but I got the gist of what he said. Stepping forward, I motioned to my fellows. "These American soldiers are going to get us some food and clean clothes. We are not prisoners any more. We are. . . I turned to the officer with a frown. "Sir, if we are no longer prisoners, what are we?"

He shrugged, "Free men. He smiled and shouted, "You're now free men!" A sergeant came up to him and whispered something. The officer nodded and turned to me. "The food trucks are on the way, kid. So's a medical truck with a doc and a couple of more medics." He frowned and looked toward the guards' barracks. "I suppose we have to feed those assholes too," he muttered, rubbing his bristled jaw.

"Sir," I asked, "are you going to food, I mean feed us with the, the…" I waved my arm in the direction in which he was looking.

It took him a couple of seconds but then he realized what I was asking. "No, no, kid, if I had my way, we'd hang those bastards right now. We may yet."

"Sir, those men only guards. They have help us. Bad guards gone away long time now. Please, sir, only boys, um, like me. Do not hang." It was everything I could remember from my schooling many years before. I likened it to starting up a rusted old motor and trying to get it working again. My mind was numb from all the new faces, the new language and now, men running around invading our spaces and giving us orders. It was a lot to absorb in such a short time. I hoped they were treating the guards well. They were our friends by now. Helmut and Karl were just farm boys pressed into service. Jurgen was a cook and had nothing to do with the killing. Riger was from a village outside Dusseldorf and, I think, nearly a half-wit - a likeable lad who forgot more that he remembered. And Hans. That's who were left of the guards, if you could call them that.

None of us knew where we were supposed to go or what we were to do once this horrible war was over. My family was dead, my home destroyed. Perhaps I would go to Palestine, like the bible taught. I remember my father toasting, "Next year in Jerusalem!" Though I barely remembered where Jerusalem was, it was as good a place as any, and perhaps without war and killing. If I only knew at the time how ironic that statement would be. I wondered what Hans would do.

It was nearing spring in southern Germany, and the weather was just starting to get warm in the late afternoons. The nearby forest was greening, and there were birds on the barracks roofs and in the trees.

"Sir," I tugged on the officer's sleeve. "What you want us to do now?"

He scratched his head and looked at the confusion around him. I could tell he'd never seen a camp like ours. I knew we were a sub-camp of the larger one at

Dachau, but his unit, I found out later, was from the 45th infantry division, which must have bypassed that hellish camp to our north. I took him on a tour of our camp and explained what each of the buildings was used for. He asked how many of us lived in each barracks. I told him that there were supposed to be two hundred and fifty men in each but now they only held about fifty. When we went into one and he saw the pallets three high, he was appalled.

Swiftly counting our pallet holes, he asked, “You mean that in each of these holes slept three men?”

I shrugged, “Yes, sir. Sometimes when a new truckload came we had four, but the SS guards, um, eliminated them quickly.”

When I pointed out the gas building, the Colonel asked, “What was its purpose?”

I described how the guards herded new prisoners into it, telling them it was for showers, but how when the doors were closed, the men in the truck turned on engines and pumped exhaust smoke into the building, and the prisoners died. Later, they just dropped in Zyklon B, a pesticide that killed quicker and used no petrol or diesel fuel. I told him that my job, with some others, was to strip the bodies, then take them on a cart to the long pit out back of the camp.

We walked there too. The last corpses were showing an occasional foot or hand where they’d been poorly covered. He shook his head, rubbing a hand across his face, the horror showing in his battle-hardened eyes.

“Does this bother you, son?” he faced me.

I shrugged. I had seen too much for it to affect me.

“How old are you?”

I frowned and tried to do the math, "I think I must be sixteen now, sir. My birthday was in the winter."

"How long have you been here?"

"Three years, sir. I came here three springs past." I hadn't thought about it in a long time. Three long years since the train dropped us in the town and the trucks brought us to this camp. I wondered if any of my friends, my classmates, or my family were still alive.

A soldier strode up and said something to the officer, whom he called Colonel. He turned to me and introduced himself as Sergeant Heinrich Small. He spoke excellent German, though he wore an American army uniform. "I am the Colonel's interpreter. The Colonel would like me to tell you how sorry he is and ask you to please come back and speak to your fellow, um, men, so we will tell you what is about to happen." He gestured for me to follow him.

I did. What else was there to do?

We walked back to the kitchen area, where the prisoners were now milling about. I shouted for them to listen to me.

I again explained how these men were Americans. "They will give us food. Doctors will treat us and help make us better." I also told them, with help from Mr. Small, how the war was not over yet and that we were advised to stay in this camp until it was safe to travel to our homes or wherever we wanted to go. Some of the soldiers would stay with us.

It sounded like a very good plan.

CHAPTER 9
Hans' Story

After about one hour an officer came into our barracks and spoke to the soldiers. A tall boy with a cigarette hanging from the corner of his mouth motioned for us to stand. Then another soldier told us to put our hands on top of our heads. He showed us what he wanted and then shoved us in a line against a wall. I felt so scared that they were going to shoot us that my hands started shaking and I think I started to cry. Helmut stood up from the table where the sergeant interpreter was questioning him. He began shouting, "Don't shoot us! Please don't shoot us!"

The soldiers were nervous and cocked their rifles. They yelled back but we didn't know what they said. Now Karl joined Helmut. They both waved their arms and walked toward the soldiers.

The interpreter jumped up and stepped between the two groups, "Stop, stop!" he told the soldiers. Then he turned and faced us. "Wait, we are not going to shoot you. These men have been ordered to search you for weapons and then take you outside to feed you. That is all."

We looked at each other, and I said, "Do we have your word that you will not shoot us, sir? Your word as an officer?"

"Yes, yes, you have my word. Just don't give us a reason to shoot you."

Once again, we put our hands on our heads and lined up. One of the soldiers patted us down and emptied our pockets. Wallets, pictures, a few coins and not much else piled on the table.

"Where is your ammunition?" the interpreter asked.

"We were not issued any, sir," Karl said. "There is a box in the Commandant's office. It wasn't necessary, except for hunting in the forest."

"You hunted them in the forest? You sick bastards." The interpreter turned to one of the soldiers, a corporal, I think and said something. It could not have been something good because the corporal's eyes narrowed and his face grew hard. I saw his trigger finger twitch. He motioned us outside. What had Karl said?

We were ordered to sit on the edge of our porch and keep our hands in our laps. Across the compound we could see three trucks that had just pulled in. I counted ten wheels on the front one. It was piled high with boxes and several soldiers unloaded it. The next was a smaller one heaped with uniforms, weapons, ammunition and duffle bags. The last vehicle had huge red crosses painted on it. I supposed it was an ambulance. Three people unloaded boxes from the rear and carried them to the vacant Commandant's office.

All the vehicles looked battle-worn but the boxes of supplies looked new or at least unused. The war had come to Kefferstadt.

The prisoners were herded back behind the fence that separated their compound from the entry gate. A table had been set up and the sergeant who had interrogated us was now talking to the prisoners one by one, probably taking down their names and home towns. Meanwhile, three soldiers, obviously cooks, prepared food on two tables set up beside the large truck. Several of the prisoners helped unpack and lay out the food. A sergeant ladled the corn mush we were going to eat into dented steel mugs. Another soldier brought the food to us.

I was puzzled. I thought the sergeant who had interpreted for us said we would be fed, but this was not fair. The soldiers had brought plenty of food. The smell was starting to drift across to us. Karl stood and asked one of the soldiers for more food. He was hit in the face with a rifle butt and knocked back onto the porch. Helmut and I scrambled to help him. Behind us I could hear the bolts on rifles slamming home. A soldier was screaming at us and suddenly a bullet punched through the door just over my head. Everyone stopped moving. The only sound was Karl moaning.

An officer ran up and pushed the soldier's rifle upward before leading him away. He yelled some orders over his shoulder at the other soldiers, who lowered their weapons. Slowly people started moving again and we helped Karl back to his place on the porch.

I ate my mush with a spoon and motioned for more. A private took my cup to the rear of the truck, filled it with water and returned it to me. So that was my first meal in captivity. I suppose it was more than the Jews had been given for their first, and for many, their last. I strained for a look at Herschel but could not see him amidst the confusion.

Just before sunset, the sergeant interpreter came up to us. He stood with his hands on his hips looking down at us. "You men will be confined to your barracks for now. You will only be allowed to come out to eat right here. You will have no contact with the men who were formerly your prisoners. In two or three days you will be taken by truck to a prison camp south of here. Once you are there, a military commission will decide what to do with you. You are now prisoners of the United States of America and Allied Forces in Europe." He looked at us with disgust and kept kicking up dirt with the toe of his boot.

I stood up. One of the soldiers raised his rifle in my general direction, "But, sir, what will become of our friends?"

"Friends?" He looked confused. "What friends?"

I gestured at the large group of prisoners now being fed by the army cooks. "The men who used to be prisoners here. They have become our friends." I didn't know if he understood what we had been going through these last several months.

The sergeant laughed and turned to one of our guards and said something. The guard snorted and shook his head. Then he turned back to me and came close. I stood half a head taller than him but he barked in my face, "From now on you have no friends. Those men are no friends of yours, you animals! I hope you get what's coming to you. You make me sick, the lot of you. Now get back in the barracks! Shnell! Shnell!*" He waved his hands as if herding a flock of geese.*

Two days later, the trucks pulled out, and most of the soldiers formed up and followed them through the gate. The ones who were left kept us inside. The next morning an open truck came for us. We were shackled and shoved up into the back where a chain was run through our leg shackles.

As we were sitting there, I heard a thin cry, "Hans, Hans!" It was Herschel. He was trying to push through the compound gate but a soldier blocked his way.

I stood and waved my shackled hands over my head. A soldier in the truck with us pointed his weapon at me. Now we were both prisoners.

"I'll find you, Hans. I'll find you," was the last thing I heard as the truck pulled out of the camp's gate and drove in a cloud of dust toward the nearby town.

CHAPTER 10
Herschel's Story

I watched the truck drive out of the camp, our guards shackled and seated on benches on either side. I don't know if Hans heard me yell to him. An American soldier prevented me from leaving our compound. I tried to push around him, but he blocked me forcefully with his rifle and insisted that I was to stay.

"If we are now free men, why do you still treat us as prisoners? Are we now prisoners of the Americans instead of the Nazis? Then nothing has changed!" I screamed in his face,

Abruptly I turned and tried to find the colonel's interpreter. Yes, the Americans were feeding us better food. Yes, their medical personnel were attending to us. Yes, they had found clothing to replace the rags we wore. But we weren't allowed to leave the former prison compound. Since Granski left, we had had more freedom with our guards than with the Americans.

After I had calmed down, I found the interpreter at the desk set up at one side of the gate on the porch of the commandant's office. He and the sergeant interpreter were discussing something, and they brightened at the sight of me approaching.

"Herschel, can you help us explain to the men here that we can't give them all the food they want? If they eat too much, they will die. They have to take their food slowly, building up their strength. Three men have already died just since we got here. One, we think, from eating too much, too fast."

"And the other two?" I asked.

The sergeant rubbed the back of his neck, "Tuberculosis, I think. I see from the medics' examinations, most of you have some sort of disease: malnutrition, rickets, lung and intestinal parasites. I could go on."

I frowned. "Is that why you won't let us leave? You have to help us get well first?"

The officer nodded. Looking down at his boots, he said, "Some of the diseases are very contagious, and we don't want you to spread them to the general population. Or, for that matter, to our troops."

"I understand, sir, and I will urge my fellows to comply. Will you tell me when some of the stronger ones can leave? I - I have no place to go now. My family is dead, except maybe a brother. He went to a different camp. What will become of me?" I felt a deep longing for my old life, but in the same vein, I didn't ever want to go back to our shop and house. How I hated those hypocritical neighbors of ours. If I could, I would take a rifle from a soldier and go back and shoot every one of those bastards.

The officer put an arm over my shoulder and walked me away from the table, whispering to me, "Herschel, I heard of a camp in Austria that they are setting up to let you rest and recuperate, and get some training. They have people you can talk to about starting over. I have also heard that some of you Jews want to go to Palestine. Maybe that's not too bad an idea, no? Your own place?"

I thought about it. 'Next year in Jerusalem'. It had a certain appeal. "Sir? Where was the truck taking the camp guards?"

"Oh, you don't have to ever worry about them hurting you again. The Allies have a big camp set up for them. Give them a taste of their own medicine, the bastards."

"That's good, sir, but where is this camp?' I didn't want him to think I was going after Hans. I had tried to explain to him two days ago about how the guards had helped feed us and keep us alive, how Hans had saved my life, but I could tell that he thought it was made up or a delusion. When he looked at me curiously, I decided to stop asking, hoping that he did not think I was a guard masquerading as a prisoner.

I then did as he asked and spoke to our fellows about the diseases and food. Most understood, but a few, Gypsies from Romania, wanted to leave as soon as possible. The major took me to them.

"Take it slowly, Milosh," I said. He was their senior, their elder. "When the doctor thinks you are strong enough, he will issue you passes and give you food. Then you can go home."

"I am strong enough, Herschel. Please, we want to go."

"Just a few more days," I said, calming him. "We are still in a war. It is not over yet. Have a bit of patience. It will be over soon, my friend."

Grudgingly Milosh agreed to wait one more week. Especially since the food was much improved.

Perhaps the doctor knew where the guards were being taken. I entered the former commandant's office and found two medics working on four of my fellows. Two lay on pallets on the floor. Beside them were chairs with clear bags hanging from them. Tubes led down from the bags to their arms. They seemed to be asleep. One was a boy I just knew as Yakov, from a town outside Munich. The other was an older man whose name I cannot remember. On the desk lay one of my friends, Ira. The medics were sponging off some open sores and attempting to bandage them but Ira was struggling.

I went to him and laid a hand on his shoulder, "Rest easy, Ira. They are only trying to help you."

He looked up with fevered eyes. "Hello, Herschel. The pain is very bad and they aren't reducing it, only making it worse. Can you talk to them, please?"

I nodded and spoke to one of the medics. He filled a syringe with a clear liquid from a small bottle and jabbed it into Ira's arm. I watched Ira's face. In a few moments, it relaxed. He squeezed my hand in thanks.

The doctor sat at a small side desk. Papers were piled upon it and a large ledger lay open before him. I stood by his side and waited for him to finish.

He finally looked up and smiled wearily. He was maybe as old as my father, thin and with a small moustache. Dark bags hung under his eyes like two plums and his uniform was disheveled. He looked like he hadn't slept in days. "Hello, son, what can I do for you?"

I smiled back tentatively. "Hello, sir, my name is Herschel Rothberg." I wasn't sure how to lead into what I wanted.

Before I could say more, he said, "Good morning, Mr. Herschel Rothberg. My name is Dr. Adelman, Sam Adelman," and he held out his hand.

I looked at the slim fingers. It had been years since I'd shaken anyone's hand. I extended mine like a child, but he engulfed mine fully, like an adult, like a man. At sixteen years, was I truly a man? I'd never had a Bar Mitzvah, the Jewish ceremony that ushers a boy into manhood.

He motioned me to a small wooden bench by the wall, and we sat down next to each other. "Sir, Dr. Adelman, can you tell me where they took the guards, our guards?" And it all came rushing out about Hans. I told him I had to see my friend, a friend who had saved my life. The bad guards were long gone and the boys who were there at the end were our friends. They'd treated us fairly and had never killed anyone. The last bad guard, Granski, had run away months ago.

He pondered this, scratching his stubbly chin. Finally he turned to me, "Son, I'll find out, but you know I have no authority to get him released. He was a guard at an extermination camp! I can get you his location, but the rest is up to you. In a week or so, I'll be rejoining our outfit for the push to Berlin. I believe that you fellows, you who want to leave, can be trucked to a place in Austria called Landesberg. The Red Cross is setting this place up for refugees and former prisoners. They are calling these camps DP camps.

Displaced Persons." Then he muttered under his breath, "My God, there must be millions of you out there."

I placed my hand over his on his knee, "No sir, not so many left. The Nazis were very efficient."

He knew what I meant and just nodded, not looking at me. "I'll find out where your friend was taken. Come back tomorrow, Herschel. I'll get one of the officers to make you up a pass so you can travel through Allied lines. I'll also see if I can get you a ride going that way. That's about all I can do for you."

I thanked him warmly and shook his hand again.

That night I slipped out of my barracks and found the rock under which Hans and I had buried the good jewelry. I unearthed the cache and wrapped the best pieces - a diamond brooch, a heavy pair of platinum cufflinks inset with large rubies, several stick pins with blue sapphires and three more pieces set with large stones - in a bandana one of the soldiers gave me. I reburied the jar. Maybe someone, many years from now, would unearth it and find the rest, a pirate's treasure.

Back in the barracks, I quickly sewed the jewelry into a pouch and tied it around my waist. The rest of the day, I helped the sergeant and the officer interview the men and translate for them.

Two days later I was in the back of a truck heading south for Austria, clean clothes on my back, pockets filled with good American food and a piece of paper with the name of the camp where the Nazi guards had been taken. Best of all, I had an official looking paper Dr. Adelman had made up. It asked other American officers to please assist me.

"I am coming, Hans," I whispered to myself.

CHAPTER 11
Hans' Story

The five of us rode in the back of the truck for three days. Fortunately the weather was dry and getting warmer. The American soldiers gave each of us a blanket and a metal dish for food, though no utensils. At night we would stop by a field and help set up a large canvas tent. The rations were cooked on two small stoves on the back of one truck. At night, the soldiers took turns keeping guard.

They never unchained us except to take us to the toilet, and that was only one at a time, often in the late afternoon, and into the surrounding forest. The soldiers treated us like vermin, pushing and shoving us with their heavy rifles. In the beginning, when the first one of us was taken into the forest, I thought we were to be shot.

The first was Karl and he was whimpering and implored me to do something. I knew he had to go badly but when he resisted, the soldier just laughed and made gestures pointing and poking him with the rifle barrel. It was the same soldier who had struck him in the face with his rifle, and he was terrified. Who could blame him?

I learned some American language on that trip. The one thing I learned was that Nazi was followed by bastard. American soldiers didn't know more than a few words of German. Shnell *was one and it was usually screamed.*

I learned to ask for water, food and clothing. The soldier who rode in the back of the truck with us was named Jimmy. He didn't like it when we couldn't pronounce the J properly. I practiced with him until I got it right. He taught me the American words for arm, leg, head, foot and some others like food and truck.

On the afternoon of the third day, we came to a hastily constructed compound that resembled Kefferstadt, only much larger. It appeared that most of the buildings had been burned and the new barbed wire fence only recently been erected as evidenced by the piles of dirt by each post. Guards patrolled the gates with dogs, much like we used to. The truck stopped by a small maze-like gate where a German- speaking American soldier wrote our names down in a book. He asked our ages, ranks, service numbers, former assignments, places of birth, heights and weights and then had another soldier take our photograph up against a piece of canvas with numbers painted on it. Then we were escorted to a tent and assigned a cot. The interpreter informed us that we'd get two meals each day, and they would interrogate us at their convenience.

I asked how many men were in this camp.

The officer sneered, "You five make just over four hundred, all former camp guards. See how you like it on the other side, Nazi bastards."

After folding our blankets and placing them on the foot of our beds, Karl and I stepped outside and wandered over to a group of some fellows our age.

"Gutten tag," I said, introducing us. Two of the other fellows introduced themselves as Heinrich Schmidt and Josef Keppeler. The others just turned away, whether from shame at being here or fear or what, I did not know.

"Where is your home?" I asked Heinrich. We walked over near the fence, where we found a crude wooden bench and sat down on it.

"I am from Berlin," he said, "though I fear that I will never see it again." His whole body sagged. He was a good-looking boy about seventeen years of age, same as my own. He also seemed to be healthier and better clothed than Karl and I, though there was a patch of blood on his tunic.

I pointed at the dried bloody patch, "Are you hurt?"

He looked down, "Ach, no. That is not my blood. One of the other guards started to run when the Ami soldiers arrived and they shot him just as he went past where I was standing. It is his blood." He shook his head. "I was not about to run after that happened."

"And where was this?" I asked him in a low voice.

He leaned in toward me and whispered, "Dachau. Can you believe it? I was only there for three weeks! All I did was help destroy papers, uniforms and things like that."

He went on, "I didn't even know what the camp was for."

This was a story I would hear time and time again. How could they not know? How could the local townspeople not know? The smell alone was awful. They say that people who live near an abattoir get so used to the smell that the brain ignores it after a while, but they still know they live near an abattoir. When I came to Kefferstadt, within a day I knew that it was no "work camp".

I chose to let this pass. If Heinrich wanted to live within this fantasy, who was I to question it? The war was coming to a close and, once again, Germany was on the losing side. My father fought in the Great War of 1917, and we lost. Now I was involved in my own generation's Great War and we were defeated. When would we learn? Our people had followed the Fuehrer blindly. No one was allowed to question him and now he had brought us to this. I asked Heinrich, "Have you heard any reports of the war or Berlin?"

"Ya. Not going well. The Amis come from the West, the Russians from the East and the Allies down from the north, you know, the British and the Canadians. I have even heard that there are Italian troops coming from the South. Can you believe that? They were our allies!"

I laughed, not believing these rumors, "Next you will be telling me that the Japanese will be fighting us too!"

He looked startled, "Have you heard something I do not know?"

I patted him on the shoulder. "Relax, my friend, I am just making something up." How much crazier could this war get?

"What else have you heard?"

"I heard our radio man say that Berlin is in ruins from constant bombings. Many of the civilians have

been killed, and the noose grows tight. It will all be over in another week or two. After that, I do not know." He grew morose again, staring down at his scuffed boots, idly swinging them back and forth in the dirt.

"Have you heard anything about the Fuehrer?"

He shook his head. "Nothing. The last time we heard was just for us to fight on to the last." He snorted, "Easy for him to say. He didn't have to get shot at." This last was said in a small whisper so as not to be overheard by anyone. He looked around furtively and leaned close to me. "There are men here who would kill me for just saying that."

I was surprised. "Aren't there just old men and boys like us here?"

"Nein, Hans. There were still almost two hundred guards at our camp when the Amis came."

"They didn't run away? Most of our guards did or got sent to the front."

"Nein, ours didn't have a chance. The Amis parachuted in and surrounded the camp before anyone could run. My friend Horst got shot because he was frightened and ran." He muttered, "I was just as frightened but couldn't move with all the guns pointed at me." He got a faraway look on his face, " The first Amis came down shooting outside the fence, then more and more both inside and outside. After awhile, trucks and jeeps came up the road from the city." He turned to me again, "The Amis are very well equipped, and very disciplined. They have been fighting here in Europe for a very long time, and yet their uniforms are in good condition and they seem to have plenty of ammunition."

"Yes, they came to our camp quickly and took charge most efficiently. However, they did not kill any

of our people and seemed to be genuinely helping the prisoners."

"Ya, they do bring their medical personnel in right away. I think this is good. Do you agree?" Heinrich asked.

I nodded, and then reflected, "Do you think they will hang us or shoot us?"

Heinrich shook his head, "Nein, I do not think so. They could have done it easily by now. I understood one of the Ami soldiers say that we would be tried by a military court."

I looked out through the wire. "What is that camp they are building? Another for our people?" I saw a large force of soldiers driving in steel posts, stringing barbed wire and putting up large tents.

Heinrich frowned and said, "I think that is for Landsmannschaft (displaced persons), you know, refugees, homeless people and," he leaned toward me and whispered behind his hand, "Jews, former prisoners. Even Gypsies!"

We stood and I decided to walk about the camp to get my bearings and see if there were any other boys I, perhaps, knew from my school days.

CHAPTER 12
Herschel's Story

After a long day riding in the truck with several wounded soldiers, we came to a small town. I don't remember the name. Many of the buildings had been bombed and the American Army officers had taken over what was left of the Rathaus, or city hall. I assisted the wounded soldiers to their medical tent, and then went looking for an officer.

I found an officer with gold leaf-shaped pins on his collars. "Excuse. Please, sir." I tapped him on the arm. He was just standing with his hands on his hips, surveying the rubble. This officer had dirty trousers tucked into his boots, a short jacket and a helmet with a red star in the front.

"Yeah, what?" he muttered without looking at me.

I tapped him again, tugging on his sleeve. "Sir, I need information, please." He was taller than me and outweighed me by at least fifty kilos. I held my pass under his nose.

"Eh? What's this?" He snatched it and read it quickly. In a second he thrust it back in my hand. "What can I do for you, kid?"

"Sir, I need ride in vehicle."

"Yeah, sure, don't we all? Where do you want to go, kid? New York?"

I frowned. New York? Why would I want to go to New York? "No sir, south. Near Austria. There is a camp there called Landesberg." Now I had to lie to this man. "I think it is for Landsmannschaft, sir." I had to find Hans, and if I had to lie, I would do it. I felt bad. In fact, I felt terrible, but if I told him that I was going to try to locate a guard from a death camp, he would have me locked up.

"Landenshafter? What's that, kid?"

"It is a camp for refugees, sir. The word means displaced persons." I thought fast. "I think my brother may be there. He is all I have left in the world."

"Yeah? Too bad. We're still fightin' a war."

Ach, was this where my search would end? I could not give up yet. "Please, sir, don't you have a Red Cross vehicle going south or a supply truck? I will ride in the rear or even on top."

He eyed me from under his helmet. "You wanna get to this here DP camp pretty bad, eh, kid?" He extracted half of a cigar from his breast pocket and lit it with silver lighter. In a moment he moved it to a corner of his mouth.

"Yes, sir. My brother may be there." I felt bad lying to this officer, but maybe I wasn't lying. My brother Isaac could be in that camp. He could still be alive.

"O.K., I'll tell you what. We've got some ambulances heading south in a couple of hours with wounded. The Army has a hospital set up in Augsburg. That's as close as I can get you. It's about ten or fifteen miles from that camp. You know the camp you're heading for was a concentration camp, don't you? How do you feel about that?"

I shrugged, "I have come from Kefferstadt, sir."

He said nothing, just looked appraisingly at me, frowning.

I felt he deserved more. "It was an extermination camp. There were fewer than one hundred of us left when the Americans came."

The officer put a hand on my shoulder, "I'm sorry, kid. It's a screwed-up world."

"Yes sir." What else could I add? Even I knew what he alluded to.

"You see that medical tent there, kid?" He pointed to the large khaki tent with the huge red crosses on fields of white painted on the canvas. I had helped take the wounded soldiers there. It was a very busy place. Though the German soldiers were nearing their end, what fighting that was still going on was fierce.

"Yes, sir."

"Well, you be in front of it at," he looked at a large wrist watch, "fifteen hundred hours. That's three o'clock for you civilians, okay?"

Since the war had started, we Germans had kept the twenty-four hour time.

"I'll see you get a ride out of here. If I'm not there, just tell them that Major McReady said it was okay." With one last squeeze on my shoulder, he pushed by me and strode into the Rathaus.

This would probably be my last ride. I went off to find some food and something to drink. A dining tent had been set up for the medical personnel, and I walked into it. Of course I used Major McReady's name and got a heaping plate of some kind of pinkish meat, mashed potatoes and some green beans from a long serving table heaped with food. Against the side wall of the tent was a table holding a large silver container full of coffee and thick mugs. I was in heaven. All this food would have fed everyone in our camp for a week.

At the appointed hour I stood before the medical tent, two apples in my pockets. The Major spoke with a thin redheaded man with the now familiar Red Cross armband, and I was motioned to the rear of an ambulance. The Major shook my hand and wished me luck.

Inside the truck were four soldiers on litters. Two had no legs, just bloodstained bandages. One was swaddled in bandages from his chest to the top of his head and the fourth had a shiny cream on what was left of his burned face. His hands were tied to the sides of the litter, probably to keep him from scratching at the wounds. He moaned incessantly. I should have been horrified, but after what I'd been through at Kefferstadt, I think I was immune to human suffering. What did that make me?

The countryside was a combination of blasted holes, toppled and burned trees and peaceful farm country. The small villages were fairly normal but the larger towns had been bombed and attacked by heavy artillery. I saw a few bodies, and, in one town, a man's corpse hanging from a street sign. In another town I saw several women being herded by a mob and pelted with stones. Their heads were shaved and their clothes torn. I heard one man yell, "Collaborator!" In almost every village and small city, American soldiers wearing armbands with the letters MP on them were acting as police, traffic controllers and generally bivouacking troops, usually in the largest and fanciest houses. To the victors belong the spoils. I would never know. I had never lived in a Germany that had won a war. The only spoils I ever saw my good German neighbors making off with were the possessions and property of the Jews.

Late the next afternoon, after getting two more rides, I stood in front of the gates of the DP camp at Landesburg. Across a wide road and dirt field, I saw the barbed wire and gates of the guards' camp. It looked remarkably like my old home, Kefferstadt. After all, it had previously been a concentration camp.

The DP camp was very busy, and all sorts of people were coming and going. While I stood before the gate, a truck pulled up and several men in black and white striped camp suits like I had worn were helped out. Their heads were shaved; they were gaunt and weak. They looked like I had, like scarecrows.

Two civilian women rushed out and told the truck drivers where to take the men. A large, tent sat inside the gate to the right. It was obviously the medical clinic. There were large red crosses painted on the roof to discourage aircraft from bombing it, either Allied or German, though I doubt that there were many Luftwaffe airplanes still flying.

As I started across the road, a motorcycle came roaring toward me. It sounded inordinately loud. A German soldier sat astride it, waving a grenade over his head. It was one of the can-shaped ones with a handle sticking out the bottom, a Model 24 *Stielhandgranate*. I knew it was filled with steel and iron scrap. He was shouting something, but I could not make out what he was saying over the roar of the motor.

The cycle hit me a glancing blow as I tried to avoid it, but I managed to deflect his arm and the grenade sailed over my head and rolled under an empty nearby truck. I covered my head and dropped to the pavement. I looked out of the corner of my eye, and saw the rider throw up his arms and fall backwards off the wildly swerving cycle. I thought I heard shots. Absently, I noted that it was a German military BMW R75 cycle, dark gray in color with white letters painted on the petrol tank.

Just then, the grenade exploded. A great blast of hot air flipped me over and drove me backward. I saw the truck heave upward and then fall slowly onto its side, the canvas aflame and petrol spilling out. I knew it was about to explode. At the same time I was peppered by numerous particles. That was the last thing I remembered.

CHAPTER 13
Hans' Story

We heard the blast that came from the front gate and ran in that direction. I bumped into Karl on the way and he gasped, "What has happened?" We ran. "Is it an air strike?"

"I do not know, Karl." A glance at Heinrich only brought forth a shrug.

Along the gate, several guards were facing us with rifles at the ready, nervously looking over their shoulders. About fifty of us crowded the fence, trying to see the street and what was happening. A cloud of smoke hovered above the street, partially obscuring a large truck lying on its side. Soldiers and civilians swarmed around a man laying in the street and, farther up to our left a motorcycle was smashed against a utility pole. I saw a German helmet still rocking in the dirt by the side of the road.

Several more men ran up and loaded the fallen man onto a stretcher. I couldn't see very well, but they were treating him as if he were still alive. I wondered what had happened.

"Do you think it was a bomb in the truck?" asked Karl.

"I do not believe so," I replied. "It looks like something happened with a soldier of the Fatherland involved." I looked around and called, "Does anyone here speak any English?"

A boy stepped near me and said, "Yah, I speak some. I spent one year going to school in London."

"Gut. Ask one of the soldiers what has happened, bitte." I grasped him by the arm and pulled him before me. He looked daunted as an older soldier shouted something at him, and he tried to pull back. I held onto his arm and urged him again, "Ask him."

"Please, sir, what took place here? Was someone killed?"

The soldier poked the rifle at us and shouted, "Some Nazi son-of-a-bitch tried to blow up the DP camp. They got him though, shot him right off the goddamn cycle!" He grinned and poked again with the rifle, "You boys git on back there a ways."

My friend asked, "Was it the soldier they were carrying on the litter?"

"Naw, it was some civilian who got knocked down by the cycle and probably got blowed up by the grenade. The guy ridin' the cycle is dead. I saw them put a blanket over him." He squinted at us, "Why? Was he a friend of your'n? Did you guys know he was comin'? Maybe to break you fellas out?"

"Oh, no, sir. We just hoped it was not an air strike."

My new friend said his name was Josef Kreisher. Karl, Heinrich and I introduced ourselves and we moved off to a corner of the compound where we squatted in the dirt while Josef explained to us what the guard had said.

Behind my back I heard one of the other prisoners say, "I wish it had been an air strike and obliterated that nest of vermin across the road." He spat in the dust. I looked at him, a sergeant major. "What are you looking at, young swine? Do you know what they are going to do to us, all of us?" He stuck his tongue out and tilted his head to the side, holding a hand over his head. "They are going to hang us." He spat again and walked off with two other sergeants.

I gulped and looked from Karl to Josef.

"Do you really think they will hang us, Hans?" asked Heinrich.

I shrugged. "I do not know." I contemplated this for a long moment, and then said, "Would you, if you knew what was done in our camps?"

Everyone fell silent after that comment.

After looking around furtively, Josef whispered, "You must be very careful with what you say around some of the older guards, my friends. Remember, they are very committed to the Fatherland and to the Fuehrer. Being captured is a blow to their pride and they look down at any of us who were just, um, there?"

"But the war is over, or nearly so. What good does it do to continue to support the party?" I asked, befuddled. That some men would like to continue to obliterate Jews was something that had not occurred to me.

Josef leaned forward again and spoke slowly, "There is a faction, at least in our camp, who took an oath to continue to uphold the Reich after the war is over. These men swore that they would infiltrate the postwar government, if the Allies even let us form a government, and keep the spirit of the Third Reich alive."

Karl just shook his head, "But to what end? They have rid Germany of the Jews, the Gypsies, the homosexuals. Who is left to attract their anger?"

Josef just shrugged, "Do not worry. They will find some new group to blame for all our troubles. If it could only be the Gestapo or the SS or even the military."

I sighed. Would this foolishness never stop? Millions and millions dead from this insane war and some want it to continue. I have to get away from this place, away from Germany. I looked at the tall fence and the guards patrolling the perimeter. Impossible. I guess that is why none of our prisoners have escaped.

Oh Herschel, where are you now? If they are going to hang me soon, now is when I need you most.

CHAPTER 14
Herschel's Story

I opened my eyes and looked up at raw wood rafters. Was I still at Kefferstadt? My head ached and the rafters blurred. I tried moving my extremities. My left toes were all right, but my leg wouldn't bend. All my fingers wiggled and my arm muscles tensed but my right arm ached. What had happened? Where was I?

A face hove into view. A woman looked at me and smiled. "Finally awake, sleepyhead?" she asked in curiously accented German.

"What happened? Who are you?"

She smiled warmly. "I am Sofie, a nurse here. And you are going to be up in no time." She patted my hand and sat on the edge of the narrow bed. Her fine brow furrowed, and I saw small flecks of gold in her hazel eyes.

"What happened to me, Miss Sophie?"

"You knocked a grenade out of a crazy man's hand. Unfortunately, you were too close to it when it exploded."

"What is the extent of my injuries? Will I be disabled?" I was in a panic. Sixteen years old and my life was over.

"Oh, *nein*," she chuckled. "You are a strong young man and will heal rapidly, and of course, we need the bed for much more seriously injured patients, yes?"

"But my leg. I cannot bend it. Is it broken?" I tried again to flex the knee. I could feel it, but it wouldn't bend. I tried again, this time harder. A jolt of pain shot up to my hip.

"No, not broken. It was dislocated and you have a bad gash on it. We have sewn up the cut and strapped your leg to a board to give it a rest. In two or three days you will be hobbling around on it. I have asked some men nurses to carry you to a tent in the nearby camp. I will look in on you, and we will send you some food each day until you are able to come to the mess tent by yourself." She patted my hand and said, "You are in a hospital, just down the road from the camps. The American military moved us into an empty warehouse building until we can get one built in the camp."

Sofie touched my leg through the sheet and smiled again, "You know, you are something of a hero, young man. If the German soldier had made it through our gate and detonated the grenade, we would all most likely be dead. For all of us I would like to say thank you, young Herschel."

"You know my name, Sofie? How?"

"In your trousers was a scrap of paper from an American doctor asking other American soldiers to assist you." She frowned and gripped my hand. "You were in Kefferstadt. We heard of it. I am so sorry. Why did you come here? So far."

Ach, I have to tell another lie. I befoul myself. "I hoped my brother Hans would be here." Why did I say Hans and not Isaac? Isaac, my real brother, I had not heard of or seen for more than three years. I had trouble picturing his face, but Hans' face I knew, I saw clearly. His close cut straw colored hair, blue eyes and funny nose with the small bump on it. Just a boy like myself really and not far, just across the roadway. How was I to get him free?

Sofie nodded, her lower lip between her teeth. "Perhaps. The camp grows bigger every day. There are more than one thousand here now and more are arriving. When you are better, go see Maria at the registration tent. She will have a list of guests."

"Guests?" I snickered. Sounds like the camps. "Are there more of the prisoners coming here?"

"Yes," she replied with a sigh. "We never expected so many. The Americans are raising tents, and then will be building barracks as quickly as possible. They are gathering the former prisoners, those who wish, of course, from all over this part of Germany and Austria."

"Gut. So, many have survived? How is that possible? Do they know how many were executed?"

Sofie hung her head and I could see tears slide down her weary face. In an almost inaudible voice, she whispered, "Millions. The last I heard was more than five million."

"Mein Got, so many." I was quiet for a long minute.

"So there were several camps?" I was curious. I thought perhaps that the main camp at Dachau and our camp were the only ones.

She laid a hand on my arm gently. "Reports are still coming in but we have had reports of more that ten thousand camps all over Germany, Poland and, in fact, all of the occupied countries." She shook her head wearily, "I fear they will find more. You know how precise and accurate we Germans are."

"Am I the last Jew in Germany?" I asked in a small voice.

"Nein, Herschel. There are many survivors here. I am so ashamed of my countrymen."

"Then you are Deutsch? From where?" I was curious about this woman. She was older than me, but only maybe ten years. Her hair was a dull blonde. She was strongly built, like my mother. She wore a wrinkled khaki blouse and a dark skirt and no jewelry that I could see.

"I moved to America with my parents when I was a girl. My father was in the export business. I worked for the American Red Cross and when I heard about," here she hesitated, searching for the correct word, "the atrocities, I insisted on coming back to help."

Alone? No family? "A husband?" I asked quietly.

She wiped a hand across her eyes, smearing the tears. "My husband is dead," she said. "He was a sailor. His ship was torpedoed. One year ago." Abruptly she stood and searched her pockets for a handkerchief. "I will look in on you tomorrow, Herschel." With that, she spun on her heel and left me.

The war. This war. Everyone has a story. Everyone is surrounded by tragedy and death. And it was all due to that damn fool, the Fuehrer, Adolph Hitler. I lay back and pulled the blanket over my head.

From the next bed came a voice, "Go on, hide under there. I will guard you."

I jerked the cover down and sat up, furious, "And who are you, swine, to listen in to my conversation?"

He grinned and replied, "I am Mendel."

"Mendel? Mendel what? What is your family name?"

He kept grinning, though it was more forced now. "No family. All gone. My new last name is Israel, for that is where I am going. To Israel, Canaan, Palestine, call it what you will. As soon as I am able." He flung back the blanket and pointed to his leg, or where his left leg used to be. It was gone from just above the knee. A clean bandage covered the stump.

"I will walk soon. They told me the people here will make me a new leg. I will become a pirate perhaps?" And he lay back laughing.

When he stopped, I asked, "Where did you lose the leg, Mendel? In one of the camps?"

"No," he replied. "In the forest, fighting the Nazis. I was shot, and the wound became infected. The Amis came, and I was sent here. So, I am Mendel and you are Herschel, eh? The hero?" He laughed his infectious laugh again. "The war is nearly over, Herschel. Why don't you come to Israel with me? We can both be heroes!"

Just what I wanted to be, a hero. "No, Mendel, not quite yet. I am searching for my brother, Hans. Perhaps when I find him, we will both go to Israel." I lay back wondering how I would free Hans.

Mendel turned on his side toward me and spoke, "We will build a great nation in Palestine, Herschel. Someday I will be the president or Prime Minister or Fuehrer or whatever they will call him. Maybe king?"

Now I laughed, "Yes, King Mendel the First. And I will be Prince Herschel!" This game playing, though fun, was tiring. I gave Mendel a wave and drifted off to sleep.

When next I woke, an elderly rail-thin man was sitting by my bed. He wore a patchwork skullcap and had the beginnings of a scraggly gray beard. I wiped the sleep from my eyes and recognized him from my camp. He was the other Rabbi. I tried to remember his name. I used to just call him 'Rabbi'. He was from Warsaw, I think.

"Horowitz," he said. "And you are Herschel. How are you feeling, young man?"

My brow must have been furrowed or he could read my mind. "They tell me I'm going to be all right, Reb Horowitz. And how are you?"

"Gut, gut. Clean clothes. Plenty to eat," he fingered his clean shirt and smiled a weary smile. "Not much kosher, but…?" He shrugged as if it were not important. "Soon you will be moved to a tent where I am in residence. I assured the lovely Sofie that I would look after you until you were walking again. Is that all right with you, young man?"

I shrugged and assured him that this was fine with me. I gestured to Mendel who was now fast asleep, "Can we bring Mendel too?"

The Rabbi shrugged, "I have no issue with that. If they will let him go, he is welcome."

Later, when she next came to check on me, I told Sofie our decision and she agreed.

Three days later I was discharged from this crude hospital, and two men helped me to the Reb's tent. Sofie carried my meager belongings. I felt my waist and the bandana with the gems was still tied there. The Reb had set up my cot on one side with a makeshift table beside it. I was still weary so I lay down after drinking a cup of cold water that the Rabbi had left for me.

The next day Mendel was brought to the tent and his cot placed next to mine. We were of an age, and Reb Horowitz had his own corner.

In a few days, under the Reb's attentive care, I began to walk, stiffly at first, then more sure of myself. Then we helped Mendel out of bed and, with a crutch the Reb acquired, we got him onto his foot. Awkward at first, soon Mendel was hopping around the camp, making friends, renewing acquaintances, trading anything and everything he could get his hands on. The lad was a natural businessman. Not only would he be King Mendel, he would probably own Palestine.

The following week, I went to see Miss Maria in the tent that housed the camp office. "Hello, I am a friend of Sofie, the nurse."

She rolled her large brown eyes and said, "Of course. Sofie has many friends. Now, what do you want?" Miss Maria was a strong woman, slightly heavy, with short dark brown hair and soft, round cheeks. I guessed she was only in her early twenties.

"Sofie said you keep the roster of guests. I am looking for my brothers Isaac and Hans."

She sat back in her battered chair and eyed me, "Isaac? Hans? My dear boy, I need much more than that to go on. Do you know how many Isaacs come here? It seems like every other man who comes through that gate is named Isaac. Can you do any better than that? Last name, please?"

I had to think for a minute. Last name? I hadn't used it in so long I almost forgot it. Maybe I should use a name like Israel, like Mendel. But no, my brother

Hans has a last name. "It is Rothberg. Hans Rothberg. Isaac too."

Maria turned to large cabinet with many wooden drawers. She rifled one expertly, then another. Finally she turned and said, "I'm afraid not, young man. No Hans or Isaac Rothberg has come through our gate. At least," she amended, "not yet." Regarding me over a pair of half glasses with a weary eye, Maria asked, "What tent number are you in? If either Rothberg shows up, I will send him there."

I told her and walked dispiritedly back to my tent. Mendel and Reb Horowitz looked up expectantly as I shuffled in. I just shook my head. Not yet, but soon.

CHAPTER 15
Hans' Story

Karl, Josef, Heinrich and I arranged with a senior guard to have us put in the same tent. He was indifferent. After we were directed to our quarters, we moved our meager belongings into it.

As a cruel joke, we were each issued two sets of the striped trousers and tops that our former prisoners had worn in the camps. The Nazi guards refused to wear these garments. Later the Sergeant Major we had seen, a man we learned was named Muller, called on us to bring out the striped uniforms. In front of the American Colonel who was in charge of the camp, some of the prisoners piled the hated stripes into a clear spot and set them afire.

There were no officers in our camp. The Sergeant Major had appointed himself as our commandant, backed up by several older sergeants, two from the SS still in their black uniforms. Many of us needed new uniforms or some sort of clean clothing. As I have said before, my shirt and trousers were from the sorting bins at the camp, but I still possessed a uniform jacket. It was torn and worn through in several places.

"Hans, where can we get some clean clothes?" Asked Karl

"I believe you mean other than those striped uniforms?" I replied.

"Yes, of course." I thought for a moment, and then said, "You fellows wait here. I will go speak to one of the guards." After I left the tent and started toward the gate, I heard hammering and sawing. This was a new sound so I walked toward it.

Some American soldiers and civilians were constructing a building near the gate. It was going to be large, I noted, and beside it was a lorry with a huge stack of boards that filled the back. I saw a short, dark haired corporal looking about, so I pulled a board off the stack and walked over to him with it on my shoulder.

He smiled and said something in American that I didn't understand.

I grinned back at him and set it where he indicated. Then I watched as he hammered it into place. Before he finished, I hoisted two more onto my shoulder and brought them to him.

The Corporal stopped and tucked his hammer into his belt. After helping me put the boards down, he pointed a thumb to his chest and said, "Pistolli. Rocco Pistolli."

I copied him and said, "Rothberg. Hans Rothberg." We shook hands. I was amazed. I was seventeen years old, a former guard at a death camp, and this American soldier, this Rocco Pistolli, a sworn enemy, had just smiled and shaken my hand.

"Hello, Hans Rothberg," he said looking into my eyes.

"Hello, Rocco Pistolli," I replied. I resumed pulling planks off the truck and helped Corporal Pistolli hold them high on the wall while he hammered them in place. The day grew warmer, and I removed my jacket. I saw the Corporal looking at what was left of it.

A shrug and more boards. As we worked, he spoke in American. I didn't understand, but he pointed frequently and named the hammer, nails, lumber, and then some clothing items. I learned fast and repeated the words back to him. He corrected me until I spoke them properly. There were other men working but not nearby.

At noon, Corporal Pistolli put up his hammer and nails and signaled to me to join him. We walked to the gate, but the tall guard wouldn't allow me through. The corporal argued with him but to no avail. Pistolli turned to me motioning toward his mouth and said a new word, "food."

I nodded vigorously and fingered my clothes. He looked me up and down. Then made a motion over his shoulder, and stalked through the gate.

I walked back to the diminished truckload of lumber and sat on the tailgate. My stomach ached and my back was weary. But the day was warm and I quickly fell asleep.

A foot nudged me awake. It was the corporal. A delicious smell wafted from a sack in his hand. We sat on the back of the truck sharing a warm loaf of bread, a wedge of cheese and a large piece of hard sausage. It was delicious. I thanked him several times. "Danke, danke." He schooled me in the American words, "Thank you."

In another bag were a pair of olive green trousers and a wool shirt. He said something again in American and pushed the clothes toward me. Again I thanked him. We sat eating the last of the bread.

Corporal Pistolli asked me several questions. I couldn't understand him, but I knew they were questions by the inflection in his voice. I smiled and shook my head.

He held up his palm toward me. He poked himself in the chest and said, "Pistolli?"

What was he trying to say? I already knew his name. "Ya," I said.

He shook his head. "Yes," he corrected me.

I frowned. Then it dawned on me what he was trying to do. He was trying to teach me American English. That was why he had been teaching me the words for the tools we'd been using. I concentrated carefully. I wanted to learn English. No, I wanted to learn American English. I saw it now. If I lived, if they didn't hang me, if I could somehow get away, I wanted to get to America. "Yes," I repeated. "Yes!"

For the next several days, I assisted Corporal Pistolli in building. He continued pointing to various things and naming them. Soon I learned a few verbs and we were able to have a stilted but two-way conversation. He told me that he came from a place called Philadelphia, which was in another place called Pennsylvania. When I frowned, he drew a squiggly line in the dirt, which, after a few minutes, it dawned on me that this was intended to be a map.

He pointed and said, "New York?"

Everyone had heard of the big city of New York, just like everyone has heard of Berlin.

Then he moved the stick down a bit and said, "Philadelphia."

We sat with our backs against the wall we'd built and I drew an outline of Germany and pointed to my hometown, just outside Dresden.

Soon he brought two more changes of clothes, which I shared with my comrades, Karl, Helmut and Heinrich. We continued constructing the building, assisted by several more American soldiers and a few civilians.

CHAPTER 16
Herschel's Story

The days went by. I walked, feeling stronger each time. Most days Reb Horowitz accompanied me. At first we spoke of our families and then of our schooling, carefully avoiding the topic of our camp. I hadn't known him well, just when he secretly said prayers or when it was his turn to help me pile the corpses on the trolley to take them to the pits. When no guards were about, he said the Hebrew prayer for the dead over the bodies. When guards were about, he silently moved his lips.

While we walked, he told me his story and I told him mine.

After a week, King Mendel started walking with us, haltingly at first but stronger by the day. He refused any and all help. One of the American doctors had procured an artificial leg for him and helped to fit it. After several adjustments Mendel was left to fend for himself. "No more crutches," he insisted

One day we came upon a pair of men digging a large hole. I stepped forward and asked in German what they were digging for.

A thin, bald man said, "A latrine, son." He stood up, hand against his lower back and eyed me, "Seems to me a strong lad like you could maybe help us?"

I looked at my tent mates and the Reb and Mendel nodded, and then walked off. I jumped into the hole and seized the shovel. Beside me a short, thickly muscled man, several years older than me with a shock of red hair and a bristly mustache just nodded toward the opposite corner. I took up the shovel and began to dig. I felt strong and soon developed a rhythm. The hole grew deeper and the dirt piles once knee-high outside were now chest-high.

"Ease up, lad. The wagon comes."

I jumped up and held out a hand for my shorter companion. He grasped my wrist and hauled himself up. A slab-sided wagon driven by an American soldier and hauled by two dispirited nags stopped by the hole.

"Well? What are you waiting for? You didn't dig that dirt out of the ground to save it, did you?" laughed the driver. He jumped from the seat and grasped one of the shovels. "Here, I'll show you how us Nebraska farm boys do it!" And he started to shovel our piles. He worked steadily and without a wasted motion.

Even though I had been shoveling for more than an hour, I stood beside him and matched him stroke for stroke. Soon it became a contest, with our companions cheering for one or the other of us. We looked at each other occasionally and grinned. It only served to spur us on. Finally the wagon was full. We collapsed with laughter and fell to the ground.

"You are a pretty fine shoveller, young man," he panted, handing me a jug of water he retrieved from the footwell of the wagon.

I drank thirstily and said, "You are not very bad yourself, old fellow." And we fell to laughing again.

"You speak pretty good English, sonny boy. Are you an American?"

I chuckled, "Oh, no, sir. I just have learned some English in my school years ago."

"Well, you are the first one I've met in this Godforsaken country who speaks good old English," he said.

"Where do you take this dirt, sir?" I queried the exhausted soldier.

His face lost its humor, "To the Nazi camp." And he pointed toward the other side of the road.

I thought for a minute. *This might be my only chance to get inside there.* "May I come with you, sir? Perhaps I can help."

"Help? How could you help?"

I shrugged. "Well, sir, I speak some English as well as German, and," I reminded him, "I am a fine shoveller."

The soldier barked a laugh and held out a hand, "Canfield, Harry Canfield."

"Herschel Rothberg, sir, at your calling." We clasped hands and shook once.

Harry Canfield struggled to his feet and helped me up, "Sure, lad, come on, but you won't have to shovel this dirt over there. Those Nazi bastards will empty the wagon."

"What is it to be used for, sir?"

"I think they're going to be using it to level a building site. I heard talk that they're building a big courtroom and are going to put the former guards on trial." He motioned me up to the seat and climbed in beside me. Clucking at the horses, he snapped the reins and off we went, slowly but toward the gate, the slow hoofbeats muffled in the dusty road.

As we passed my tent I saw Mendel and the Rabbi seated on boxes outside. They rose as the wagon passed. Mendel started to raise a hand but the Rabbi restrained him. I just nodded at them. I think the Rabbi guessed where we were heading and why. He must have known of my relationship with Hans. Most of the prisoners from Kefferstadt did.

At the gate to the Nazi camp, the guards questioned Private Canfield, asked who I was and where we were going. He replied that I was just a civilian helper. They let us in and locked the gate behind us. Two guards followed behind.

All about were men in Nazi uniforms. My stomach tightened. Though I was now a free man, the sight of those arrogant, terrible men still made me fear for my life. We came to the building site and stopped at one end. Men were waiting. I climbed down with Private Harry and sat in the shade. Two Nazi privates climbed into the wagon and slowly started slinging shovels full of the black dirt into a depression near the rear of the partially completed building.

Though I kept my head down, I looked at each prisoner carefully. No Hans. I stood and stretched. As I started toward the opposite end of the building, Private Canfield shouted, "Stay close, Herschel. Don't leave my sight."

I smiled and waved, "I will not go far, sir." I stuffed my hands in my pockets and strolled on. As I came to a doorway, a man came out and nearly bumped into me. I instinctively reached my hands out and gripped his arms. It was Hans.

His eyes grew wide and he gasped, “Herschel!” What…?”

“Shhh,” I whispered, shoving him roughly back into the doorway. Inside the room, we hugged each other briefly. After these months and the long rides, now I had found him, my friend, my brother.

“Where are you now, Herschel? How did you find me?” Tears were streaming down his face as he clutched my arms. “They mean to hang us.” He hung his head down, not looking me in the eye.

“Then we have to get you out of here.”

“Escape?” He asked.

“Yes.” I gripped his upper arms again. “I’ve been thinking about this day. You have to get out with as many of the other guards as you can. They will cause a diversion. When they run away, you must run for our camp.”

“Your camp? Then you are at the DP camp across the road?”

“Yes. I am in a tent with two friends, a one-legged boy named Mendel and Reb Horowitz from Kefferstadt. Can you get out of here?”

“I do not know. I will try. When?”

I thought. “Two nights. It is a quarter moon and will be dark. Come to the fence on the west side of our camp about one hundred meters from the corner by the street. I’ll be waiting there near midnight.”

“Yes,” he said again. “I will be there.” Then Hans pushed me hard out through the door.

I stumbled out the door and would have fallen, but Private Canfield caught me. He glared at Hans and then helped me back to the wagon.

I heard Hans curse me in German. I almost laughed, covering it with a cough. Canfield helped me up into the now empty wagon.

"I told you to stay where I could see you. Do you know what these Nazis did for the last few years? They were guards at the death camps." He went on without waiting for an answer from me. "The rumor mill says that this building is going to be a courtroom. That end," he pointed to where we had dropped the dirt," is where we will hang the lot of them."

"Yes, I understand, sir. I am sorry." The wagon was empty now and the two American guards with weapons stood beside it.

Private Harry motioned the horses and wagon forward and I sat quietly, my demeanor peaceful but my mind going a million kilometers per hour. How was I to get Hans out? Even more important, how was I to pass him off as my brother?

All I could do is wait by the fence and hope he would be able to come.

CHAPTER 17
Hans' Story

I was overwhelmed seeing Herschel. I had thought I would never see him again. I was sure the American military courts would hang us all. Now, I might have a reprieve. Herschel had it worked out, a plan to free me, I hoped. To free me, but what of my friends? All I could do was help them get through the fence. After that, they were on their own. I knew I must make a plan to free myself from this camp. Herschel could only help me after I was on the outside.

The fence was the problem. The Americans had built a very tight compound. Around our camp was a fence made up of many strands of barbed wire, taller than my head. There was a gap of possibly three meters and then another barbed wire fence, just as high, surrounding the first fence. If we walked to the front of our camp near the gate and looked across the street, there we could see the other camp, this one surrounded by a single fence, not as high. I'd heard it was a camp for displaced persons from all over the Reich.

I went to our tent and got Karl, Josef and Heinrich. We walked the fence line, stopping behind a large canvas tent in the rear, and I whispered to them, "I am going to escape from here in two nights. I am not going to wait for them to hang me for something I did not do."

Karl looked at me, shocked, "If the Americans catch you, they will shoot you. Are you insane?"

"Yes, Hans, you do not know if they will hang us. Don't they have to give us a trial first?" asked Josef.

Josef was the youngest of us, barely sixteen years, short with curly black hair and a slender build. His father had been a fighter pilot and Josef had not heard from him in more than two years. His mother and two younger sisters had lived in Dresden. None of us mentioned what happened to that poor city. He was naïve, had only been in Dachau two or three months before the camp was overtaken by the American soldiers.

I rounded on him. "Every man here was a guard at a camp that killed thousands of innocent people! You think the Amis care about a fair trial? Do not be a simpleton."

Karl grabbed my arm, pulling me back. He stood at my side and said to the others, "Hans is right. Any trial will be a farce." He looked from one to the other, "I will go with you, Hans."

I felt a hand gripping my shoulder. Karl and Heinrich and Josef stiffened, almost standing to attention.

A voice behind me whispered, "So, young man, you and your little friends are going to try to escape?" The Sergeant-major came around and stood before us, hands on hips. He had on a clean uniform, a tall cap and a sneer on his face. He was much older than any of us, with short, graying hair, a deep scar under one eye and thick wrists. A tattoo of a chain was around one of those wrists. He laughed, a short bark.

"I, I don't know what you are talking about, sir."

"Oh, come, come now, young private. I overheard everything you said." He eyed me as if he were used to using a monocle, "And just how do you propose getting through the wire?"

I pulled my shirt up slightly. Tucked into my trousers was a wire cutter. I let the shirt drop. "I was helping a soldier on the new building and found these. One of the working men must have left it behind." I shrugged. "I thought that I would need it someday, perhaps."

He held out his hand, "Give."

"Nein," I replied, stepping back.

The Sergeant Major came at me and attempted to grab the cutter, and I slapped his hand away. He looked at me in amazement. Once again he came at me and I struck him in the stomach with all my force. He expelled a huge rush of air and clutched his sides, nearly falling.

I'd held my ground against this supposedly superior non-commissioned officer. The other lads moved up beside me and stiffened. "The night after this one, I am going out through that fence there." I nodded toward the fence as it ran behind the large tent. "If you want to escape also, be here after midnight. The moon is small then, and it will be quite dark. If you have two or three others, bring them with you."

He nodded and smiled craftily, chagrined, hoping no one had seen a private strike him.

"You are not my superior any longer. The war is over, Sergeant-Major."

"No, not yet, Private. The Fuehrer may still survive. Survive to begin again."

I shook my head, "No, sir, our war is kaput, again. I suggest that if you get out of here, you just disappear. That is what I am going to do." I turned to my mates, "Come, let us go plan." I turned one last time to the older man. "Remember, midnight, tomorrow night. Good day, sir."

Back at our tent, I assisted Karl in removing all insignia from what was left of his uniform. Since we were not allowed knives, we used a small piece of glass Karl had found on the ground near the construction site. We worked methodically removing the epaulets also and mending the blouse as best we could.

"Are either of you fellows coming with us?" I looked at Josef and Heinrich.

Josef shook his head, looking at the floor. "I cannot, Hans. I am too afraid. I am sorry." He looked up with a tear in his eye.

"Heinrich?" I queried the taller boy. He looked from Josef to me. I could almost see the wheels turning.

Finally he stood. "I'll come too. I do not like it here." He put a hand to Josef's shoulder. "You will be all right, my friend. You are young and Amis will see that."

The next night was cloudy. Even better. We were all tense. We had been sitting on our cots for hours, speaking quietly of our homes and families. No one had a watch, but Karl assured us that it was time to go. I did not know how he knew but we were all eager to depart. We had reconnoitered the camp the last few days and knew that the area behind the large tent in the rear was the darkest and least guarded. We hoped the Amis assumed the barbed wire fences would discourage any attempt at escape.

Josef wept openly as he hugged each of us. He kept mumbling over and over how sorry he was. We assured him that we understood. Heinrich clutched the small bag of food we'd managed to put aside, and Karl extinguished the small lantern we had been issued.

"Let us go, my friends. We'll meet again in Stuttgart." I slipped out the tent flap into the darkened compound, staying in the shadows. A few stars shone here and there between the clouds. I waited for my eyes to get accustomed to the dark. Against the sky I could see a watchtower in one corner of the compound. Atop it, two moving red dots suggested soldiers smoking.

In a few moments we reached the large tent. I felt, rather than heard, the lads behind me. I stood quietly by the rear tent corner. A voice hissed from the other side.

"Is that you, Private?"

"Ya. Just wait until the cloud covers the moon," I hissed back. A few minutes passed. As soon as I saw the edge of the moon darkening, I moved quickly to the fence and knelt, feeling for the wire. The lowest strand parted with a nearly audible twang. I felt the barb on the second wire and snipped between it and the next. I felt the third but couldn't feel the barb. I ran my hand back and forth. No barbs. Curious. Had they run out of barbed wire? No, the next was barbed. Just as I was about to snip it, a large hand reached out tore the cutter from me.

"Let me do that, you clumsy boy." The Sergeant Major quickly snipped the bare wire before I could warn him. I saw a flash of light as the searchlight came

on and a deep voiced siren began to moan. He had cut a trip wire connected to an alarm system. The Sergeant roughly shoved me aside, and he and two more men pushed past and into the gap between the fences. It would take the American guards some time to find the break in the fence, I knew, but that still only gave us seconds.

"Come," said Karl, lifting me to my feet and pushing through the cut wire. Ahead I saw the next fence wires were cut and the older men were running for the nearby wood.

"Go!" I pushed Karl, then Heinrich through the fence as the searchlight swept in our direction. I barely had time to run the opposite way, toward the other fence corner, toward the road. "Good luck," I whispered at my friends.

Parked ahead was a truck with one axle on a stand. I threw myself on the ground beside it, hoping that the searchlight would pass over me. It did, and I immediately jumped up and ran for a small clump of bushes. They cast a dark shadow offering cover. Behind me I heard the pop, pop, pop of a machine gun opening fire. Before me I heard jeeps roaring out of the compound. When I took a chance and looked up, I saw soldiers with weapons at the ready. The drivers growled through the gears. I quickly covered my head, not wanting my pale face to expose my position. The searchlight swept over them and momentarily stopped, making sure it was American soldiers in the jeeps. I knew that they would be blinded for a few seconds and that the area outside the light circle would appear darker than the surrounding landscape, so I drew myself to my feet and ran again. Behind me I heard screams as some of the heavy bullets found their marks.

I hoped that it was not Karl or Heinrich for they were good boys and had never harmed anyone.

The road lay like a pale streak before me. I crawled toward it, then rose to my feet and deliberately walked backward, hoping that anyone who saw me or my footprints in the dust would assume I was walking toward the disturbance, not away from it.

In a minute I was across the road and running alongside the fence, opposite the direction my comrades had run. I dared to stop and look behind me. The spotlight illuminated a broad swath of the open ground between the fence and the nearby wood. One jeep had stopped, and soldiers with lanterns were inspecting the cut wires. Other soldiers were looking at crumpled shapes, and at another, a soldier knelt and was attending a wounded man who was screaming. I hoped again that the wounded man was either Karl or Heinrich or that they had escaped.

Lights were coming on all over both camps. Up ahead a hand waved through the fence. "Hans, Hans, here!" A voice hoarsely whispered, trying to be quiet.

I ran and stopped by this disembodied hand. It pulled me down to the ground.

"Hans, crawl under here." Herschel had a long pole, which he was using to pry the wire up from the ground. I squirmed under, and he helped me to my feet.

We watched the action across the road. The fence line was well lit by spotlights and running soldiers who held hand lanterns. I saw some soldiers wrapping two limp bodies beside one jeep.

"Come," Herschel said, pulling on my blouse.

I became Herschel's brother Hans that night.

CHAPTER 18
Herschel's Story

I grabbed Hans under his arm and helped him to his feet. In the dim moonlight we embraced.

"Thank you, Herschel," he said simply.

We stepped back into the shadows and watched what was happening across the street. A jeep carrying a single wounded man sped back toward the road, turned left and sped toward the medical clinic I had been released from a short time ago. A medic bent over the rear where a stretcher was secured. We couldn't make out the wounded figure or his attire.

"Was that someone you knew, Hans?"

He shrugged, "I do not know. I hope not. I mean, I hope my friends were not the two bodies they are loading now." A 4x4 truck had come out and slowly made its way to where the bodies lay. We saw several soldiers climb out of the truck and begin to hoist them inside in their blankets.

I pulled on Hans' arm. "Come, we need to lose you in the camp."

Silently we slipped from shadow to shadow. Near the front of the camp, a crowd had gathered trying to see what was happening in the prison camp across the road. We skirted the rear of the crowd and found my tent. Inside, Reb Horowitz and Mendel were reading a book they'd borrowed from the small library the Red Cross people had started. The Reb had reverted to his role of teacher, as both Mendel and I were eager to continue our schooling.

I entered the tent, tugging Hans in behind me. Mendel looked up, and then struggled to his feet, or rather, his foot. The artificial leg was propped against his bunk. Reb Horowitz cocked an eyebrow; his spectacles perched on the end of his nose.

"My friends, this is my brother, Hans." I shoved him before me and into the light of the kerosene lantern.

Reb Horowitz turned it brighter and squinted, looking up. "I know you," he said.

"Yes, sir, you do." Hans sat heavily on the edge of my bunk and leaned forward toward the old man. "I am Hans Rothberg. I was a guard at your camp. I am sorry, sir, for everything I did there."

I interrupted them. "Reb, Mendel, Hans saved my life. Now I have to save his. I need your help. We both do."

The Reb studied him, and then said slowly, "You arrived only a few months before the Americans came. The gassings were over by then, were they not?"

"Yes, sir. I had no part in that, nor would I have."

"Do you remember when Sergeant Granski shot the three cooks in the kitchen?" I asked.

The Reb nodded.

"I was there. Granski was just about to shoot me when Hans here stepped between us. I am alive because of a camp guard." I took a deep breath. "He is now my brother. I ask you both to accept him."

The Reb looked at each of us, at Hans the longest. "How old are you, young man?"

"I am seventeen years, sir. Why?"

"I want to insure that you have a long life, my son." He held out his hand, and they shook. Now he looked at Mendel and nodded.

Mendel held out a hand, though with some reluctance, "If Rabbi Horowitz and Herschel say you are a good man, then I also welcome you." He grinned. "I am Mendel."

He gestured at the tent. "Such as it is, this is our home. Tomorrow we will get you some new clothes and papers. Then? We shall see what the future will bring." Mendel brightened. "Perhaps you will come to Palestine with us?"

"First you will have to make me a Jew, Mendel!"

I laughed. "That is a job for the Rabbi here. He is trying to make good Jews of all of us."

The Rabbi shrugged. "It is my job." He waved a hand, peering at us with mock severity. "Sometimes a curse."

Mendel and I grinned. We'd not been the best of students.

Hans said, "I have just escaped from the camp across the road with two friends, and several other men. Two were killed and one was wounded. I hope that my friends are all right. Do you hate us?"

The Rabbi carefully replied, "It is for God to decide if you are a hateful boy. We can only forgive. Are you worth forgiving?"

Hans frowned, "I never killed or hurt anyone, sir. What the Reich did was wrong, and I will try to make up for that."

I indicated Mendel, "And you, Mendel?"

"I do not know enough about what went on in your life, Hans. Right now I will have to trust Herschel's word. Over the next weeks, we will talk, and then I can make up my mind. Until then, your secret is safe with me." He held out a hand, and they shook.

The next day, I walked down to the main tent with Hans. The American woman I had met before, Maria, was at the desk. I stuck a big smile on my face and took Hans by the arm. "Excuse me, Miss Maria? Do you remember me? Herschel?"

She frowned, studying me, then Hans, "Of course, I do. Herschel, uh, Herschel…"

"Rothberg, Miss Maria. I have found my brother, Hans. He has been here in the camp for more than a week."

Her frown deepened, "I don't remember you coming in, Herr Rothberg. Do you have your papers?" She held out a hand.

Herschel and I had rehearsed this before we came. "I am sorry, but my coat with the papers inside was stolen yesterday." He hung his head, "I am sorry, Miss Maria. I would have come sooner, but when Herschel and I discovered each other, we just spent the night discussing the past few years."

You could see her soften, the frown fading. She scribbled some notes on her large pad and filled out some cards for her file before making out a green card with Hans' name and description. It would allow him to come and go in our camp, eat in the mess tent and get some clean clothes from the supply office.

We thanked her warmly and turned to leave. Just as we got to the doorway, she called, "Rothberg brothers."

We turned apprehensively. We had almost made it. Had we been caught? Would Hans now be sent back across the street? I said, "Yes, Miss Maria?"

"Will Hans be staying in your tent with you?"

I just nodded.

"Then I suggest you get another cot from supply for him." She smiled and cocked an eyebrow. "So I'll know where to find you. If I need you, of course."

"Of course. Thank you, Miss Maria." I said.

"And, Herschel, have you found your other brother yet?"

I gloomily shook my head, "Not yet, Miss Maria." And we left.

Standing outside the tent, I whispered to Hans, "I think she knows something is not right. We must be careful." He nodded.

We stopped at the supply tent and were issued a folding cot, bedding, a metal cup and clothing the Amis had confiscated from local civilians. Hans received a very nice pair of dress trousers, a pale yellow shirt and a waistcoat. Next we found him some shoes, brown brogans. We thanked the gaunt woman standing behind the counter. I glanced down. She had a tattoo on the inside of her lower arm. An Auschwitz survivor.

I helped Hans carry everything back to our tent. Mendel and Reb Horowitz had made room for him next to my cot. Between us was a small table and another lamp. These were new and I was amazed what Mendel was able to acquire in the camp.

I complained to him, "What, Mendel? No books?"

He grinned and swept my blanket back. Two books lay under it.

I hugged him warmly. "Thank you, King Mendel. You will be Palestine's first Prime Minister, at the very least!"

Hans smiled and gripped his shoulder. "Thank you, my friend."

"All right, gentlemen, please finish what you are doing so class can begin." Rabbi Horowitz was in full teacher mode.

After setting up the cot and arranging the bedding and clothing, we sat attentively awaiting the Rabbi's instructions. "Young men, as long as you are in this tent, we will be having instruction for at least one hour a day in various subjects. Since I am no secular teacher and am not very good in mathematics, we will discuss history," he ticked these off on thin, crooked fingers, "the Talmud, morality, ethics and almost anything else we feel is necessary." He looked at each of us and we nodded in turn.

The Rabbi cleared his throat and leaned forward. "For today, I would like to discuss this unfortunate war. We'll call today's class, the 'Morality of War'. Or maybe I should call it the 'Immorality of War'?"

For the next hour, the discussion went back and forth between the Rabbi and each of us, voicing our opinions and observations on this and past wars.

Reb Horowitz concentrated on the Nazis' dehumanizing the Jews, Gypsies, homosexuals, Communists, labor leaders and others to the point where good men, and here he indicated Hans, could commit unspeakable acts. "If they had asked their soldiers to deal out horrible deaths to their friends and neighbors, there would have been a revolt, a mutiny. However, it was because the government of the Reich conducted a systematic campaign to declassify these groups as less than equal humans, as subhuman, that the atrocities were able to occur. Without that campaign, the Nazis would never have been able to commit the acts they did." The Rabbi raised a finger for emphasis.

Hans nodded, "I know what you mean, sir. In the Hitler Youth, every day the instructors would tell us how the Jews were taking over our banks and how the Jews were killing German babies in their rituals." He shook his curly head, "I knew Jews. I had gone to school with some Jewish boys my own age and never saw anything wrong or different with them. But I knew it must be true, or our leaders wouldn't have said these things." Here, Hans, my brother, stopped and covered his eyes. He was crying now, the sobs racking his slim frame.

The Rabbi laid a firm hand on his head and muttered a prayer of forgiveness.

I looked at Mendel. He also had tears in his eyes.

"I am so sorry, my friends, so sorry. Even my father told me these terrible things." He looked up in anguish, "How could they all be so wrong? How could they do those terrible things? No, how could we have done these things?" Hans sniffed a couple of more times and wiped his wet face on his sleeve.

"Reb Horowitz, Mendel? How could we all have done the things we did or let them happen?" I was as bewildered as Hans.

Reb Horowitz had a much broader range of experience than any of us and told us his story. "I was born in Russia before the turn of the century in a town called Smetyko. My father was a butcher and bred mules while my mother raised three sons. When I was only thirteen years old, some Cossacks came into town drunk and killed several men who dared to oppose their pillaging. One was my father, and suddenly my brothers and I were now the town butchers. My oldest brother, Feivel, became the mule breeder. My next brother, Leib, and I operated the shop. We were fast learners and our modest prosperity allowed me to continue with my rabbinical studies. After all, to become a rabbi is what all good Jewish boys strive for. Despite continued pogroms," he continued," the shop flourished. Feivel also began selling mules to the Russian Army. Ironic, no?"

The Rabbi went on, "Leib married, and then Feivel. Soon the house grew too small for the boys, their wives, my mother and me. I was now twenty and with a heavy heart, I packed a bag and boarded a train for Poland. In my pocket I had the name of a distant cousin in a town near Lubin. A cousin of my mother.

"The local rabbi, an elderly man, helped me complete my training and in only two years I became the town's rabbi when he died. The congregation grew, and in due course, the Yenta found me a bride. Her name was Rayna, and she was short, chubby, blonde and bubbly. I loved her so much," he sighed, then chuckled. "I was tall, skinny, bearded and serious. We were quite the odd couple. Did I tell you that we were the pride of the small Jewish community in a corner of Lubin, Poland? Well, we were for many years."

The Rabbi was openly weeping now. After a few moments, he sighed, wiped his eyes, scratched his beard and continued, "Rayna died in childbirth along with the baby, a boy, our first after trying for a long time. I just fell apart. I packed a bag and began wandering, wandering, wandering." He snorted, "It is good that Jews, no matter how poor, are always willing to take a rabbi in, feed him, and then, of course, send him on his way. You know the Yiddish word for what I was?" He looked from one to the other of us, eyebrows raised. "No? A *shnorer*. Means a freeloader. I walked through Poland, western Russia and into Germany, until I was picked up by a squad of brownshirts near Munich, and taken to a work camp. After a while, I was sent to Dachau, then Kefferstadt where I met you boys." He smacked his hands down on his thighs and said, "That is my story. Now, could I have done anything to change the course of the war?"

We all shook our heads no. No one could have stopped the Nazi juggernaut.

CHAPTER 19

Hans' Story

The Rabbi, Mendel, and most of all, my dear friend and brother Herschel, endeavored to make me a Jew in as quick a time as they could. We studied for an hour in the mornings and two or three hours each evening. I learned all about traditional holidays like Passover, when the Jews left Egypt. They taught me about Hanukkah, when the temple in Jerusalem was destroyed and only enough oil was left to keep the eternal lamp burning for one day, yet miraculously it lasted for eight days. There were so many rituals and ceremonies to learn and remember.

I especially liked the Yiddish language. Many of the words were similar to German, so I found it easy. Words like bupkis (nothing) and chutzpah (nerve), ferklempt (choked up) and klutz (clumsy) were all similar to my native German. These words, which derived from Hebrew and High German, with some French and Italian thrown in for good measure, we started using on a daily basis. Yiddish is sometimes referred to as a polyglot language.

We talked of the history of the Jews, the wanderings over the centuries. I heard of Masada, where the Jews fought against the Roman troops and, rather than surrender, chose to commit suicide. The Rabbi knew the tales of the early Hebrews, the Assyrians, the Egyptians, the Persians and all the other people who influenced Jewish culture.

Whenever Hans, Mendel and I ate in the mess tent, we talked of the day's lessons and the Rabbi. Other boys from the camps, survivors, orphans, fellows like us, gathered around Herschel and especially Mendel. We told them of our lessons and soon the Rabbi had a full tent. Each day one or two more fellows came to hear his animated dissertations. I think he liked the attention. The first half hour or more were the Rabbi's lectures. Often the lectures were based on the previous day's questions and discussions. Soon we had to move our meetings to the mess tent to accommodate all who wished to attend.

One day we might discuss our past, another our existence in the camps. Then the Rabbi began steering the lectures toward morality and ethics. He had a difficult time convincing some not to go down the same road as their former captors. Their overwhelming desire was to hang every camp guard, every SS man and especially every Gestapo agent.

"Doesn't that make you as bad as they are?" asked Rabbi Horowitz one day, arms outspread, a puzzled look on his face.

"No!" shouted several angry young men, survivors from the death camps. One fellow stood shaking his fist. He was small and thin, a redheaded boy from Dachau.

"Do you know what they did to us? Do you know how evil those men are?" He was shaking, and his face was crimson, "If I had a gun, I would kill every one of them!" Several cheered his words.

"What is your name, son?" asked the Rabbi gently, sitting in his folding chair. He stroked his growing beard absently, crossing his legs.

"Tevi, sir."

"Well, young Tevi, it is my job, my calling, to dissuade you from this feeling."

Tevi was dumbfounded. His mouth moved, but no sound came out. Finally he was able to say, "You want us to forgive them, to forget?"

Rabbi Horowitz shook his head, "No, son, never forget. Tell your children and their children but don't let it ruin the rest of your life. Live your life to honor those who have passed away. Live an honorable and giving life, just the opposite of the Nazis." He was in full lecture mode now. "Let the Americans and British and Russians take care of the Nazis. They will be treated as war criminals. But we, we must survive and go on. We must not ever let the rest of the world forget. We," and here he was on his feet, glaring at us, "are what is left of the world's Jewry."

"Rabbi, we have suffered so much. Will it ever end? How much suffering must we endure?" Asked Tevi, anguished.

Reb Horowitz laughed a harsh laugh, "My young friend, you have not suffered. You have experienced pain, much pain, but pain is inevitable. However, suffering is a choice! Do you choose to suffer? Or do you move on?"

Tevi was perplexed, "Choice? You think we had a choice? The Nazis gave us no choice."

The Reb shook his head, "No, you do not understand. You have to choose *whether you will suffer or not. Oh, yes, the Nazis inflicted pain, but it is up to you how you use that pain. You can give in and make yourself weak or choose not to suffer, to be strong, if only inside."*

Now he continued, "We must travel to all nations of the world, settle down and show people that we are just like them. We love and laugh and work and raise families just like they do. Where you go is your choice."

Mendel struggled to stand, leaning on his crutch. "I am going to Palestine where we will establish the state of Israel," he shouted, face wreathed in a huge grin. "There will be Jewish policemen, shop owners, street sweepers, carpenters and cooks." Hoping to lighten the tense mood, he laughed and said, "There will even be Jewish thieves, burglars and bankers." He made it sound like a golden land of all Jews.

Herschel stood and, in mock indignation, looked sternly at the others, "Not bankers, Mendel!" He shook a finger in Mendel's face. " That's what got us into this mess in the beginning!"

We all laughed. I looked around, suddenly sober. I was one of them, yet I was not. As the discussion continued, I drew Herschel aside.

"What are we doing here, Herschel?"

He shrugged, "Living, Hans, just living. Why, what do you mean?"

"I mean, we walk about, we eat another's food, we sleep in someone else's tents and beds. I am used to doing work for my keep." I was walking in tight circles now, giving voice to my innermost thoughts, thoughts that had been swirling in my head for several days. "This camp is just a way station, just a place for us to

gather our wits, eat some proper food, heal and decide where we will go. I do not wish to be a refugee or a DP forever."

Herschel stopped me, "Well, I understand. What do you wish to do?"

I had considered this. "Let us approach the Amis or the people who are in charge of this camp and see if we can do some work. Perhaps there is kitchen work or building or even digging we can do. I want to learn a trade. I thank you for teaching me about gold and gems, but I do not think that is of much use now, here."

Herschel clapped a hand on my shoulder, "You are right, Hans. That working sounds like a good idea, my brother. Tomorrow we will go see Miss Maria.

"Miss Maria? I thought we wished to avoid her."

Herschel shrugged, then smiled, "My father once said, 'Keep your friends close and your enemies even closer!' I believe the saying came from a fellow named Machiavelli."

I was astonished that he'd read The Prince. *We had studied it in school. A Jew had heard of Machiavelli? "You think she is an enemy?"*

"No, she's just curious about us. So let us show her some brotherly love!" said Herschel, always the optimist.

CHAPTER 20
Herschel's Story

That evening, we discussed our plan with the Rabbi and Mendel. The Reb agreed it would be good for us to work, to feel that we were part of an organization doing good, for a change.

The next morning, as we ate breakfast in the mess tent, an American officer came in and addressed us. He strode to the front of the huge space and raised a hand. I will never forget his words,

"Gentlemen, today is May 8, 1945. General Eisenhower has accepted the unconditional surrender of all German forces fighting in Europe." With a small smile on his clean-shaven face, he uttered the words I had been hoping to hear since I was a young boy. "The war is over."

A great cry went up throughout the tent, and soon the whole camp, as the word spread. Men jumped up and hugged each other, shouting, screaming and dancing, some crying and others just smiling. We had survived. We had survived!

I sat and listened to the din, and remembered my parents, my brother, Isaac, and my sister, Miriam. I wondered what we were supposed to do now. Would we be evicted from the camp if we no longer needed the protection of the Americans? Our country was in shambles, our civilian population broken and demoralized. And the Jews? The Jews had been decimated. We had heard that millions had been killed. Millions! I hadn't even been aware that we numbered in the millions. Were we expected to return to our former homes? Amongst those who'd turned us over to the Nazis? My neighbors, who'd injured, raped and killed folks like my parents and grandfather?

No, I decided. I would never return to that town. There was nothing but hate and anger for me there. The Rabbi was right. I must leave all that behind. But where was I to go? To Palestine with Mendel? I didn't really want to be surrounded by other survivors, others who would talk endlessly about their time in the camps, the brutality, and the killings. No, I wanted to go someplace where I could disappear, start a new life and just be myself. I chuckled, be myself? I didn't even know what that meant anymore.

Hans and Mendel looked at me curiously. "Are you all right, Herschel?" asked Hans.

"Yes, Hans, I am fine."

He smiled, "The – War – Is - Over!" He threw his arms around Mendel's shoulders and mine.

"Come, let us go see Miss Maria. I have a great urge to hug a woman!" He shouted.

Hans and I walked to the main receiving tent, arm in arm, nearly skipping.

The tent at the entrance was in chaos. Cars and trucks on the road honked their horns, men and women whirled arm in arm and even the soldiers grinned at us and raised their thumbs up. We elbowed our way into the packed tent. Miss Maria stood behind her table guarding her records from the crowd. When she saw us she gaily waved, and we pushed our way toward her.

"Good morning, Miss Maria," I said holding out a hand.

She looked down. Then she laughed and drew me into a great hug and kissed me on the cheek. "It is a great day, no, Mr. Rothberg?" She held me out at arm's length. Wisps of her auburn hair were plastered to her sweaty forehead but she never looked more beautiful. It was the first time I'd seen her smile. Her entire face lit up as if the sun shone. She looked over my shoulder and saw Hans standing there and smiled.

"And the other Mr. Rothberg. Hans, I believe?"

Hans smiled shyly and came closer. He was almost as tall as I but stronger, more filled out, more of a man. " Indeed, it is a wonderful day, Miss Maria." He too held out a hand and she took it shyly, and then drew him into a long embrace, kissing his cheek.

I raised an eyebrow.

She winked at me over Hans' shoulder and said, "I have heard what you boys are doing for Rabbi Horowitz." Now she stepped back and folded her hands across her bosom. "I am proud of you two, Hans, Herschel. Please call me Maria."

I frowned, "What do you mean, Miss, I mean Maria?"

She smiled slyly, "The lectures. The mess tent. You have given that old man new life. You, and you, young man," she indicated Hans, "whether you realize it or not have inspired him. I have stood in the rear and watched him lecture and then answer all of your questions." She smiled broadly, showing even, white teeth. "And for that, I am truly grateful to you."

"Why are you grateful?" I asked. Her remark was perplexing. It seemed to me that there was more to Miss Maria than merely being a bookkeeper and check-in clerk.

"It is my job, Herschel." She looked at me curiously. "Don't you know what my full job is here?"

Hans and I looked at each other. "No. We assumed you did what we've seen you do. You know, check in the people as they come to the camp."

She laughed a throaty laugh, covering her mouth. "I am all of that, but I also am trying to find homes for all of you. I oversee the hospital records. I help provide all of you with papers, passports, visas, and I order food and bedding supplies. Soon we will start building dormitories to replace the tents." She paused and shook some papers from her table in my face, "And that is a lot of responsibility, my young friends." She drew herself up and almost theatrically proclaimed, "I am one of the main representatives of the UNRRA."

"What is the UNRRA?" I asked, having never heard of this organization.

"Why, Herschel, whose food are you eating? Whose beds do you fellows sleep in? Whose clothes do you wear?" She smiled and said, "The UNRRA's, that's whose. The United Nations Relief and Rehabilitation Administration."

"We are classified as refugees, then?"

She nodded, "Yes, refugees and displaced persons." She waved an arm, "This is a displaced persons camp."

Hans nodded, "Herschel and I have something that we would like to discuss with you."

"Discuss with me? Now? Why?" A frown creased her young face. "Is something wrong?"

"No, no," I reassured her. "Hans and I would like some work, something to do all day long, a trade, perhaps." I sought to calm her fears. "Now that the Rabbi is busy with his classes and Mendel, well, you know Mendel. He is always busy. Hans and I find ourselves restless."

She appraised us, a finger to the corner of her mouth. We were young and fit and, with the resilience of youth and the plentiful food supplied by the Americans, had regained some of our weight. "I'll tell you what, I'll see if I can find something for you to do."

"That would be wonderful, Miss Maria," agreed Hans. I just nodded and smiled.

This night we celebrated in the mess tent, which was crowded with boys and men. One fellow had a violin and another a balalaika and a third had a hand-carved flute. A Gypsy man turned over a tub from the kitchen and thumped it with his bare hands. We danced and sang until we grew tired, then stumbled back to our tents and fell asleep.

That night I dreamed about the camp, Kefferstadt. It was the first time since we had been liberated that I had dreamed of it.

In my dream, I watched a long procession of trucks enter the camp and stop by the stone building. The backs of the trucks were filled with naked people, hundreds in each truck, jammed together. All of them were moaning. Just moaning. The trucks backed up to the doors of the gas building and the backs tilted up and all the people just slid down and into the building. The doors slammed shut and then the gas trucks started up and poured their poison, Zyklon B, into the building through great flexible hoses. After a few minutes, several of us ran to the doors tugging our carts. As the doors swung open, the bodies came tumbling out. We worked as fast as we could to pile the bodies on our carts, the guards yelled at us to work faster, whipping us with great long whips I saw some Australian drovers use in a movie once.

I ran from cart to cart extracting gold teeth with a long pliers and stuffing them in a bag hanging over my shoulder. Beside me was Sergeant Granski, the cruelest of them all, hitting, punching, pulling hair. One boy hauled a cart with an impossibly high load of bodies. After a dozen feet, one corpse fell off, though he didn't see it. Granski ran to him and screamed in his face, then pulled his pistol and shot him in the face, two, three, four times. The boy's head exploded and bits of skull and brains flew everywhere. The last thing I remember just before he was shot was him looking at me and winking. It was my face that looked back at me.

I must have screamed because the next thing I knew, the Rabbi was sitting on the edge of my bed and holding my shoulders, "Shhh, shhhh, Herschel, it was just a bad dream."

Mendel looked up from his bed, and Hans stood next to mine. "Easy, brother, easy." His hand was brushing my hair back from my forehead, which was damp with sweat, though it was not yet warm outside.

"What were you dreaming about, my son?" asked the Rabbi.

I shook my head, "Nothing, nothing, the camp, the dead, Granski. It was all jumbled." Was I going to experience dreams like that for the rest of my life? "It will be all right." And I fell back into an uneasy sleep.

Morning came, bright, sunny and warmer. As it is written, 'It was the first day of the rest of our lives.'

I rolled over and saw Mendel sitting up in his bunk. He was reading, his lips moving a bit. "Psst, Mendel, what are you reading?"

He held up the book so that I could read the spine. It was in English by a man named Mark Twain. *Huckleberry Finn*. "What is this book, Mendel? You read English?"

"Yes, a little. I am teaching myself. Another man at the mess tent has been helping me. He says he used to teach English language at the university in Heidelberg."

From the other side of the tent I heard Hans say, "My father went to school in Heidelberg."

"No, Hans, our father went to school near Kassel. We: you, me and Isaac went to the yeshiva in our town. That is a school operated by the rabbis. Remember that, please."

Hans mumbled something, and I strained to hear. He was saying yeshiva over and over.

I got up, stretched and slipped into my trousers and shirt. I went to Hans, "You must be careful, Hans. Jews were never allowed to go to the university at Heidelberg. You must only talk of this when we are sure we are alone."

Hans nodded, but I knew he felt bad. "Will I ever be able to mourn my family?"

The Rabbi proposed, "Perhaps tonight, when the four of us are together, I will say the prayer for the dead for you, for all of us who have lost friends and family. Would you like that, Hans? And you boys?"

"Yes, that will be a good thing, Rabbi," sighed Hans. "Will you teach me that prayer?"

"Yes, of course. It is called the Kaddish."

"The Kaddish. I will learn it and say it every night to myself," vowed Hans.

"We will say it with you, my brother," I said.

Mendel agreed.

The Rabbi looked pleased. "We may soon have to start a yeshiva here," he reasoned.

"You already have one, every day in the mess tent." I answered, laughing.

CHAPTER 21
Hans' Story

Two days passed. Reb Horowitz continued with his private lessons for Herschel, Mendel and me in our tent for an hour in the mornings. Then he would gather his papers and go to the mess tent, where he would lecture for another hour. The discussion would continue until lunchtime. We usually accompanied him and thoroughly enjoyed his talks, as did the hundred or so men and boys, who were his students.

On this day his talk on morality continued. "My friends, how do you each see yourselves five and ten years from now?" He sat in a comfortable chair Miss Maria had provided for him. A large glass of water sat on a small table beside his elbow.

He raised his eyebrows, "You see, we have lived through a most terrible war which has taken our friends, family and yes, entire towns and cities. But you," and here he pointed around at the assembly, "you have survived- to do what? Will you become revenge seekers, like my young friend Tevi here? Or will you attempt to put all this behind you?"

He stood on shaky legs and challenged us, "Or will you settle somewhere and find a wife, and even have children? Ask yourselves, if when those children grow up, do you want them to look at their father as a murderer or as a saintly man?" Here he grinned, "Of course, to find a saintly man amongst you will be like finding a kindly Gestapo agent, but," and here everyone laughed, "wouldn't you rather teach your children that you survived a terrible time, a time of mass killings, but perpetrated none yourself?"

A hand went up in the audience. An older man shuffled to his feet and said quietly, "I was in the Warsaw Ghetto, in Poland. I have killed Germans, killed to feed my wife and colleagues. Will I ever be able to face decent people again?" He was a gaunt man, with thinning hair and a beak of a nose.

"How do you feel now, my friend?" asked the Rabbi quietly.

He shrugged and said, "Hollow, empty, useless."

The Rabbi came up to him and said, "You must fill all that hollowness with love: love for the Lord who saved you - for what, we do not know; love for your fellow men, and a love of life." Here he took the man by the upper arms and gently smiled, "I, too, have lost everything, seen my fellows gassed and thrown into pits, my wife and child dead, but I go on and so must you." He squeezed the man's arms. "Perhaps you will go to Palestine with my young friend Mendel and become one of his dreaded bankers!"

The man, whom I later learned was named Dov Lemko, looked at the Rabbi respectfully, "Do you think I can be a whole man again?"

The Reb shrugged, "That is up to you. You are alive. You are standing here. Surely God has some purpose for you." He turned to his audience. "You are all alive while others died. Surely there must be a reason. Would you waste that life God has allowed you to have? Would you dishonor those who died? Because if you throw that life away, that is what you do."

The discussion continued, with many fellows contributing fantasies of where they wished to be in those long-off five or ten years. It was obvious to me that the Rabbi's words had caused many men to look within themselves.

As the bell rang announcing lunch, Miss Maria entered the tent and caught Herschel's eye, waving him over. She stood with a large American soldier.

"Boys, I'd like you to meet Chief Hawk. He's with the 69th Seabees. That's the construction battalion assigned to this camp." Herschel and I shook the giant man's hand.

"Pleased to meet you, men." He appraised us, his eyes noting Herschel's rather slight physique and my heavier one. "Maria here tells me you want to learn a trade. Is that right? Think you can do construction work?" He spoke to us in rather stilted German.

Herschel spoke up, "I speak much English, sir, and my brother Hans here, speaks some and is a fast learner." He smiled a winning smile, "Your German is very good, sir. Where did you learn?"

He smirked at us and shook his head, "I lived in a mostly German town back in upstate New York, and I studied it in school. Never thought I'd have much use for it though."

Miss Maria interrupted, "You fellows figure things out. I have to get back to work. I hear that there are several truckloads of refugees coming in today from the east, ahead of the Russians." She waved and winked at Hans, "Bye now."

The soldier turned to us, "Men, I am Chief Petty Officer Albert Hawk. My job here is to replace the main tents with buildings. I have only ten men in my command, so I am supposed to use men from the town. I..."

"Chief Hawk, Herschel and I would like to work with you to learn this trade. We can get more men from the camp here, many who are also trained as electrical men, plumbers and builders." I had no idea if Jews were even trained in these trades but I did not wish to work with locals. They would be collaborators, former party members and most likely former soldiers hiding from the Americans.

"But I can just go into town and hire experienced men." Was the Chief arguing or testing us?

"Hire?" Herschel blurted. "But Chief, the people here will work for nothing. We already get food and a place to sleep from the UNRRA. Many of these men would just like to have something to do during the day. Do you really want former Nazis working for you? Your enemies?"

Before Chief Hawk could answer, I jumped in. "Give us two days and let us bring some men to meet you. If you are not pleased with them, then we will not object for you to hire men from the town." I held out my hand. "Are we agreed?"

Hawk considered, "All right. You bring me ten men tomorrow right here after lunch, and we'll put them to work. But," he admonished us, "if they don't work out, I have to get townspeople. I have a schedule, you know." With that he gave us a mock salute and walked out.

I whirled on Herschel, "Mein Gott! Herschel, where are we going to find ten men who will be able to do the work?"

"Relax, Hans, we have a thousand men, more, in this camp. Surely there must be some who have the trades. We just have to find them."

There were over two hundred men eating lunch right now. We rushed up to the Rabbi and put our problem to him. He nodded, understanding immediately.

In a moment, he mounted a bench at the nearest table and banged a mug on it for quiet. "Achtung! Bitte!" As the vast tent fell silent, the Reb quickly told the men what we needed and asked them to spread the word, admonishing them, "Ten men only for a start. Perhaps woodworkers and masons. Later electrical men and plumbers. Tomorrow, after the noon meal." He smiled down at us, "Anything more?"

I shook my head, and the Rabbi thanked the men and told them to continue eating. We helped him down from the bench and went to eat also.

CHAPTER 22
Herschel's Story

That night, the four of us sat in our tent while the good Rabbi quietly said the Kaddish. The almost forgotten words whispered in the night air. They were comforting, and if I closed my eyes I could remember my Rabbi from home saying the words when my grandmother died.

We fell silent and Hans wept. He just sat while the tears ran down his strong cheeks. I went to sit beside him, putting an arm around his shoulders. After a few minutes, he wiped his face on his sleeve and asked, "Why do you not weep, Herschel?"

I thought for a moment, "It was a long time ago, my friend. I think I wept all my tears away. There are none left."

Across the tent, Mendel nodded, saying nothing. Then he brightened, "I almost forgot, comrades, I have presents for you both." He rummaged in a bag he had acquired and pulled out two knitted yarmulkes. These were skullcaps worn by Orthodox Jews worldwide. Grinning, he handed them to us and exclaimed, "Wear this, Hans, and you will officially be a Jew!"

I agreed, "Once you place this on your head, there is no going back." I enjoyed teasing him.

Hans turned it round in his hand, examining it, "You know, I used to see these on the heads of children I played with as a youngster but I never knew what they were. When I was in the Hitler Youth, we used to knock them from the heads of every Jew we saw. I never thought I would wear one." He looked round at each of us, "I will spend the rest of my life atoning for my sins as a foolish youth." He placed it on top of his head, and I helped him move it to the back.

"There, you are now Reb Hans!" This brought a laugh from all of us.

The Rabbi leaned forward, "You know, young Hans, accepting the Jewish faith is not to be taken lightly. With the responsibilities comes great danger, as you know."

Hans hesitated, "I am aware of that, sir, and decided some time ago that I would convert, not just to save my life or for Herschel but because it is the right thing for me to do." He patted the skullcap and added, "That is, if you'll have me?"

The Rabbi stood and solemnly placed a hand on Hans' head, "By the authority vested in me by, well, me, I now declare you an official Jew." He turned to me and said, "Herschel, you may now kiss the bride!"

We all laughed, and each had a small glass of wine from a bottle that Mendel had somehow found.

The next day, after the Rabbi's lecture on self-sacrifice and helping ones' neighbors, I heard a commotion outside the mess tent.

Chief Hawk came striding in, straightening his uniform. He strode up to Hans and me and said indignantly, "What the hell is going on, you two?"

I frowned and said, "What are you talking about, Chief? We've been here with the Rabbi waiting for lunch."

He grabbed me by the arm and dragged me to the doorway. Pushing the flap aside, he pointed at the huge crowd outside, men jostling each other, trying to get to the front. As soon as they saw us a cry went up in several languages, "Me, me!"

The Chief quickly lowered the flap. "I almost got killed on the way in. Do you mean to tell me they are all tradesmen?"

I shrugged, at a loss, "I don't know, sir. Let me talk to them. I will find out." I turned back before going outside, "What trades will you need first?"

He thought for a moment, "Carpenters and cement workers."

Meanwhile, behind us, men still inside, started to move toward the Chief and Hans.

As I left, I heard the Chief mutter, "What a SNAFU."

Outside, I waved my arms for attention, "Men, men, who among you is a tradesman?"

Almost every man raised an arm.

"Sheiss," I mumbled to myself. "I need cement workers over here," I hollered pointing to my left. "Carpenters and woodworkers over there, to the right." Groups of men and boys moved to each side, leaving a large number in the center.

"The rest of you, we will call you when we get to your specialty." I went to the first group.

"Who is a cement worker here?" Every hand went up. I walked down the line and selected one fellow, "You, what experience do you have?" He was at least twenty years older than me, slim from malnutrition, yet strong looking with curly hair just starting to grow in. A lumpy, bulbous nose and puffy, scarred ears, gave his face character.

"I built three synagogues and several brick buildings in Dusseldorf and Frankfort before the war," he explained. Then he hung his head, "I also helped build ovens in Bergen-Belsen. I'm sorry." He mumbled, "I did not know what they were for until later."

"I understand, my friend. Would you select five more good men and bring them inside when you are done?"

He nodded. I told him my name, and he said his name was Sam Katz. We shook hands and I walked to the other group and found an older man who described some of his past work. I also asked him to select five men and bring them inside.

In the tent, the Chief and Hans were compiling a list of the men before them and their trades. The Chief looked exasperated. He was talking to a cadaverous fellow, bald with a croupy cough.

"Buddy, I don't need a furrier, or a teacher. I need good, strong carpenters." Finally he eased up and, with Hans translating, said, "Get well. Get that cough taken care of and then come back. We'll see if we can find something for you."

The man grinned toothlessly, and bobbed his head in thanks.

I told Chief Hawk what I had done and he sighed with relief. "Hans, would you please get a list of names of the men who will be working for me and their trades? We'll start tomorrow morning at the main tent near the gate. Zero seven hundred sharp!"

The next morning, while the Rabbi taught, Hans and I met Chief Hawk by an open space that had been cleared near the gate and the main tent. He had a roll of drawings in his hand and behind him stood a table made of planks set atop saw horses.

"Good morning, men." He shook our hands and then indicated two men in blue denim trousers and lighter blue shirts standing behind him. They both wore dark blue caps. "This ugly mutt here is Nowicki. You can call him Pete. This other guy is Nate Rosen. Yeah, he's a Jew. The only one I could find with some training." He unrolled the drawings on the table, placing a stone on each corner. Behind us, the selected men milled around, waiting for instructions.

"Okay, we're going to build a one-story frame building with a cement floor and a corrugated metal roof. It's going to be eighty feet long and twenty feet wide. You got that?"

I looked at the drawings and did the arithmetic in my head. Approximately 24 meters by six and a half meters. I looked at Hans and could tell that he was doing the same thing.

"Could we bring Mr. Sam Katz up to look at these drawings, please?" I asked innocently. "He is our best cement worker,"

The Chief frowned, "What? You don't think my guys know what they're doing?"

"Oh, no, not at all, sir. But if you are going to use these men, it would be better if they all knew what we are going to do. Besides Mr. Katz will be able to explain to the other men, and there will be less confusion," I hastily reasoned.

"Okay, okay, bring him up," sighed the Chief.

"Sam," I beckoned. When he came to the table, I showed him the drawings.

He looked at them and shrugged. He spoke to me for a few minutes in Yiddish and waited while I translated. "He says that it looks pretty easy. The forms first, some men to mix the cement, unless you are going to truck it in. He says it looks like about fifty cubic meters of cement." I turned to the Chief and his men. "Is that correct?"

Nate was scribbling on a piece of paper with the stub of a pencil he kept behind his ear. "Yup, that's about right, Chief. Guy knows his shit." Nate was a short, fireplug of a man with curly black hair, bushy eyebrows and a tattoo of an old sailing ship on his left forearm.

A Jew with a tattoo? How unusual, I thought.

The other fellow, Peter Nowicki, was about my height but heavier, older and with a large belly that hung over his belt. He seemed to have a cigar stuck in the corner of his fleshy mouth at all times. He had the brightest blue eyes I had ever seen.

Both men were good-natured and not nearly as taciturn as the Chief. But the Chief had the responsibility, and they just followed orders.

Soon, Nate was speaking with the cement workers and Peter was unloading some long lengths of lumber from a truck. Hans went with the lumber, people and I stayed with the cement workers. In short order, Chief Hawk had a device out on a tripod and had men hammering pointed pieces of wood into the ground.

After about one hour, Miss Maria came out and asked if she could borrow Hans for a short while to move some files. After wiping the dust from his face, he gladly went with her. I went with my fellows and unloaded bags of cement from another truck. We stacked them on slabs of wood and then covered them with a large canvas tarpaulin.

"We should have a mixer here tomorrow morning, men. The forms should be ready, and we can start pouring." He indicated several shovels and said, "Give me a trench about a half meter wide by about a half meter deep around the edge, will you?"

I was about to translate for Sam Katz, but he told me that he'd already explained that this was called footer and the men were already going to their jobs.

I just looked at Chief Hawk and Nate and shrugged.

The Chief came over to me and clapped a big hand on my shoulder. "You've done a good job picking these guys, Hersch. This building ought to go up easy." And it did.

CHAPTER 23
Hans' Story

Miss Maria came and got me from the worksite. Mr. Peter had just explained that the lumber we were unloading was "liberated" from the yard in the nearby town and would be used for the forms to delineate where the cement would be poured. One of the other men explained that we would spread it in sections and put pieces of iron or steel mesh into it for strength.

"Come, Hans. I would like some help with these new cabinets." She indicated four large boxes in a row by the office partition.

"I will uncase them and wipe them down, Miss." I looked longingly at her. Miss Maria was not a tall woman, but sturdy, as a good German woman should be, like my long-lost sister. She had brown hair pulled back and tucked behind each ear. I liked that she wore trousers, quite unusual at this time.

She stood leaning on the wooden partition while I used a small pry bar to uncase the filing cabinets. "Are you going to go to Palestine, Hans?" she asked.

I stopped and faced her, "I do not think so, Miss Maria. Herschel and I would like to go someplace where we can just be two people who came back from the war and wish to continue our lives."

"And where do you think that will be?"

I shrugged, "Perhaps America. Perhaps Canada, though I hear that it is very cold there." I sat on the top of one box and smiled at her. "And where will you go after you are finished here? Back to America to your family?"

Maria looked at the floor. In a small voice, she said, "I have no family anymore. My husband died in the war, and my parents passed away while I was young. My grandmother raised me, and now she is dead also."

She seemed so distraught that I went to her side, took her in my arms and stroked her hair. She stiffened and then started sobbing into my shirt. I just held her and whispered that everything would be better soon.

Maria looked up at me, and I could not help but lean down and kiss her softly. I had never kissed a woman before and it was quite different from the kiss I had once stolen from my sister's friend, Karen. Then Maria put her arms around my neck and kissed me back for a long time, pressing her body against mine.

A voice called from the other side of the partition, "Maria, are you back there? There are men coming in."

She broke away and dried her eyes on a scrap of a handkerchief she took from a pocket in her trousers. "I, I'm sorry, Hans I...."

I held both of her hands and said, "I am not. I will be here whenever you need me, Miss Maria."

"Hey, Maria, you coming?" The voice called again, this time more urgently.

"Be right there!" she called brightly. Hesitating for another second, she quickly kissed me on the corner of my mouth and ran out.

That was a very different turn of events than I expected. Much food for thought, I mused as I uncased the rest of the cabinets. As I was gathering up the wood scraps and cardboard, I heard a man's voice, louder than the others. It was a voice I thought I recognized. A voice from the past, from the camp.

I peered around the corner of the partition. Mein Gott, it was Granski, in civilian clothes. Thinner and scruffier, but I recognized that voice and those wild eyes. I listened as intently as I could.

He was fawning over Maria, "Yes, Miss, I am a Jew, yes, from Camp Kefferstadt. I have been hiding in forest for long time." Granski's German was more broken than I remembered.

She said something I didn't hear. Then he replied, "No, no, all comrades dead. Nazis kill them all. I only man left." He attempted a grin. Suddenly his gaze lifted to mine.

I jerked back. Had he seen me? Would he have recognized me? I ran out the rear of the tent to find Herschel.

Chief Hawk stopped me, "Are you finally coming back to work, kid?"

"Yes, sir, but I need to find my brother, Herschel, right away. It is very important, sir."

He looked about and said, "He's probably with that group over there, digging the last corner." He indicated three men knee-deep in a trench with three others standing and laughing at some small joke.

"Thank you, sir. I will be back in one minute." I ran toward Herschel. What would I tell him? I had been thinking of telling him about Miss Maria, but now I had a much bigger tale to tell.

I skidded to a stop and reached down and clutched Herschel's sweaty shirt. "Herschel, Herschel, you must come out now. I have something very important to tell you."

He tried to pull free, saying, "Hans, we are engaged in a contest and I am winning!" Again he tried to pull free.

I clutched tighter and nearly lifted him out of the trench. "Come now!" I shouted in his face. He must have seen the fear in my eyes because he handed the shovel to one of the other men and scrambled out.

I dragged him over to the other side of the worksite, out of range of the other workmen. "Something very bad has happened, Herschel."

He frowned and slowly unclasped my fingers where they were still gripping his shirt. "What, for God's sake? What is wrong? You look like you've just seen a ghost."

"That is as good a description as any. I was just in the main tent with Miss Maria. Some new refugees had arrived. I thought I heard a familiar voice so I peeked around the corner." I gripped Herschel's upper arm tightly. "It was Granski. And he was passing himself off as a Jew!"

Herschel was stunned, as stunned as I. He stood there with his mouth trying to form words but nothing came out. Finally he was able to ask, "Are you sure?"

I nodded and replied, "Yes, it was he."

"Mein Gott in Himmel, we must tell the Amis. He cannot get away with this."

"No, you must not," I said in a panic. "I think he saw me. If we tell on him, he will tell on me. No, we cannot tell anyone."

Herschel ran a hand through his hair, deep in thought, "But you never killed anyone. He has killed many. I, myself, saw him shoot those three in the kitchen, and he was one who ran our people into the gas building." He was frantic, "We have to do something!"

"Wait, wait. We cannot make a decision now. Let us go talk to the Rabbi." I had him by the arms again. "Herschel, you are the brain. Think. How are we going to solve this?"

He pulled free and barked, "I am thinking. Wait, we must keep calm. Let us finish our work here." He took a deep breath and tried to calm down. "Hans, I will not let them take you back. We will run if we have to."

In two more hours, we had finished our trench for the footings, and the Chief told us that we were done for today. Tomorrow we would mix and spread the cement. In the meantime, his men would go back to the town and acquire some steel mesh or reinforcing bars.

Only once did Miss Maria come back out looking for me. I spoke to her for a few minutes and told her I would be back here tomorrow. She asked me to come back this evening after mealtime, but I told her that Herschel and the Rabbi and I had something very important that we had to do.

She was curious but nodded coolly, "I understand, Hans. Perhaps I will see you tomorrow?"

"Yes, yes, Miss Maria. Of course. I will be working with Chief Hawk right here. Now, please, I must go." I took her hand from my forearm, squeezed it and Herschel and I walked as fast as we dared to our tent, all the time looking for Granski.

Reb Horowitz and Mendel were playing chess on a small set and looked up as we rushed in.

"Good afternoon, gentlemen," said the Rabbi looking from one to the other of us.

We sat on my bunk side by side. Herschel started, "Rabbi, something awful has occurred." He went on to tell him about the arrival of the hated Granski and how he was passing himself off as a Jew.

The Reb was startled, but Mendel just looked puzzled. "Who is this Granski?" he asked. "I have heard you mention him before. Is he a friend of yours from the camp?"

Now it was my turn to look startled. "No, Mendel, he was a guard. A Pole the Nazis enlisted to help in the camp. Only he helped more than the SS. He was one of the most evil guards there. Before we were liberated, he shot three men, stole some food and fled."

"So how did he end up here?"

Herschel shrugged, "I do not know. I thought he would have fled east to Poland but the Russians must have pushed west and he would not wish to be captured by them. Anyway, here he is and if we turn him over to the American soldiers, then he will tell them that Hans was a guard also."

Mendel took it all in, pondering, "But Hans saved your life, did he not?"

"Yes, I did" I said, "But the Americans will not care. I was a guard, and I escaped. They will shoot me just for that." I hugged myself. "Oh, what can we do?"

"Take it easy now, Hans. If Granski saw you, he knows that you are here the same as he is. He will not say anything as long as you do not." Herschel tried to soothe me.

"Nein, Herschel, I do not wish to put you in danger. I must flee." I leapt to my feet and started throwing my few possessions into a pillow sack. If Herschel and I were caught, he would be branded a collaborator for trying to help a death camp guard escape.

"Wait, I will come with you," he said, and rose to assist me.

The Rabbi stood and gripped both of our shoulders, "Just slow it down, the two of you. This does nothing to solve the problem of Granski. Once he knows there are others from Kefferstadt here, he will flee himself."

We stopped and sat again. "But we are the only three, are we not?" I asked.

The Reb shook his head, "No, I have seen two others here. They just started coming to morning classes. One is Mandelbrodt, who was in my barracks, and the other is Minski, the Russian. For all I know, there may be more." He held out his hands to us, "Maybe one of them will inform the American soldiers?"

"Can we take that chance?" Herschel stood and began pacing, smacking his fist into his hand.

"For now, we will have to. We will have to see what develops," Reb Horowitz' words calmed us.

We slept fitfully that night.

CHAPTER 24
Herschel's Story

In the morning we talked some more and decided that we could do nothing without exposing ourselves. The Rabbi and Mendel would try to locate Granski's tent and would watch for him. Meanwhile, we would continue building the structure under the guidance of Chief Hawk, Petty Officers Nowicki and Rosen and the workmen we had recruited.

I worked under Mr. Rosen and Hans worked for Mr. Nowicki. He was from a city called Chicago, and he talked often about something called 'the loop'. I believe it was a place, not a thing. At noontime, we sat in some shade, and Miss Maria had a volunteer bring us some sandwiches and fruit from the mess tent. Now that the war was over, the Americans had ships coming from America with much food and, once empty, they were taking soldiers back home. The first to go were the wounded and convalescing. Next were the longest serving combat troops.

As soon as possible, the men of the Seabees, who were the engineers, had come from their base in England just to build this camp and others. We did not know it at the time but this DP camp would be in use for many years.

Soon we had recruited a dozen more carpenters, and the building rose rapidly. Once the cement floor had dried, we built long walls flat on it and had dozens of men help hoist them vertically all at once. It was a beautiful sight to see, a twenty-five-meter wall go up all in one piece. In two days, the other walls were up, and Miss Maria and some of the men and women she worked with drew a plan showing how they wanted the building divided.

Every once in a while, she would come to Hans and say, "Hans? Would you please come help me move some desks?" Or, "Hans, would you please come help me unpack some cabinets?"

He would smile and say, "Yes, Miss Maria, as you wish." He'd go for an hour or two and come back out of breath, sometimes deeply flushed. I was worried that she might be working him too much, though we were working very hard on the building also, and the days were getting warmer.

All this time, Chief Hawk would show us the detailed drawings of the building; explain what each symbol meant and how to distinguish various materials from their outlines and texture drawings.

When it came time to construct the roof, Petty Officer Nowicki had us build a platform and put it on wheels. It stood more than three meters high and held two people comfortably. The lumber for the roof rafters was cut to length, and a sturdy board was designated as the first peak beam.

The Chief waved to us, "You boys get on up there on that platform. You're going to hold up that peak beam, hand the end to the guys on the end of the building, and those other guys will hand you the rafters. You nail them into the peak beam and we'll get them nailed into the top plates, you got that?"

We had seen the drawings at noon meal and Mr. Peter had explained in detail what we were going to do. Hans helped me to the top, and two of the workmen handed us the long beam from the end. The lines on it were clearly marked in pencil, with a large X on the side to which the rafter was to be nailed.

Hans hoisted the beam onto his broad shoulder and the first rafter was handed to me.

"I've got it!" I yelled and, trying not to jostle Hans too much, I nailed it in place. "Hand me another." One came from the other side, and now we had a roofline. As we nailed the rafters in place, workmen crawled along the tops of the walls nailing those ends in place also. Two men pushed the platform along slowly, and we progressed down the length of the building. *Mein Gott*, working overhead like this was horribly stressful.

"Stop, please, I need a rest," I pleaded. My neck and arms were aching.

Peter Nowicki laughed, "Look, kid, we're feeding you good American food, giving you good tools to work with and a trade. You want a rest? Rest when you're done!"

Mr. Peter was always joking with us, kidding us and laughing. The Chief was much more serious and Mr. Rosen, well, he was a Jew like me and just did his job. He once asked me during a noon meal, what it was like in the camp.

I said, "Picture the worst thing you can ever imagine human beings doing to one another. Then multiply that by ten or maybe one hundred. That is what the concentration camps were like." I began by telling him of the gas house, the trenches, the trolleys and how we were stacked in the barracks. I could tell he was shocked.

But he just nodded, not meeting my eyes. Finally he looked up and said, "I heard that they gassed and killed more than one million people at that Auschwitz camp in Poland. I can't even conceive that many deaths. Mostly Jews too, huh?"

"Yes, in our camp were mostly Jews but some political prisoners and also some Roma."

"Roma? What's that?"

"Roma. Gypsies, wandering people. They travel in wagons all over Europe. I think they originated in Romania is why they're called Roma."

"Why did they kill them? Were they fighting the Germans?"

"Oh, no, they were just too disorganized to fit into the Nazi mold. They didn't conform. Besides, they weren't Aryan." I laughed. "Most Roma looked like Jews!"

Rosen frowned, "Do I look like a Jew?"

I held my hands up, "What does a Jew look like? You are fair like Hans and yet I, his brother, am darker. My sister Miriam was dark like me, and my papa was tall and fair."

My mind flashed to Granski who was stocky and dark, unlike many Poles I knew. I'd tried to not think about Granski. We had not located him but had not become complacent.

The building continued over the next two weeks, and Hans and I filled out, becoming more muscular. Mendel sewed belts for us to hold our hammers and nails, and the Rabbi massaged my back and shoulders in the evenings. Sometimes Hans came back to the tent with us, but many evenings he excused himself, and we didn't see him until bedtime.

One day he confided in us that the next day was his birthday. He would be eighteen years old. I was proud of him and the work he did. Reb Horowitz held a hand over his head and said a blessing for him. Mendel just smiled, but we knew something was afoot.

That evening Mendel came back to the tent visibly shaken. "Please, come, my friends. I have something to tell you." He sat on the edge of his bed, his hands shaking. "You know that man from your camp, Herschel? Hans?"

My heart sank, "You mean Granski?" I asked.

He shook his head, "No, for him I am still looking. The one I mean is Rolf Minski. You said one time you knew him. Is that true?"

The Rabbi nodded, "Yes, I knew Minski. A Russian Jew." He frowned, a hand to his chin, "I believe he was a tailor or made shoes or some such."

Mendel nodded vigorously, "Yes, that's him. He worked with leather." He took a deep breath, "Well, he's dead."

"What? How?" I was incredulous. In the camps we were used to death coming daily, but here in the DP camp, it was unusual.

Mendel was near tears. "They found him strangled in one of the latrines this morning."

Hans asked, “Was he robbed? Wait, no, of course not, he had nothing. We have nothing worth stealing.” This was puzzling.

Reb Horowitz was shaken also and sat heavily in his chair. “I know why he was killed and by whom.”

We all wheeled and looked at him, waiting,

“Well, why? Who?” I asked.

The Reb’s ashen face looked up, “It is my fault. After morning class yesterday, I spoke with him and Mandelbrodt. At one point he looked at someone in the crowd and grew excited. I couldn’t tell who it was. I don’t see so well anymore. He said he thought he saw someone who looked like Granski in the rear of the tent. I tried to calm his fears and thought I had.” He shrugged resignedly, “I suppose I didn’t.”

“You mean Granski killed him because he recognized him?”

“Who knows? But, yes, my son, I believe that is what happened. Now I fear for Mandelbrodt. One of us must warn him.” He struggled to his feet.

Hans placed an arm on his shoulder, pushing him back into his chair. “No, sir, Herschel and I will find him.”

“I will go, too,” urged Mendel. “I think I know where his tent is.”

I strapped on my tool belt and stuck my hammer in its loop before we left. Hans hefted a stout piece of wood we used to tighten the tent pegs after a rain. I didn’t realize how much the camp had grown since I’d last taken a walk through it. There must have been five thousand residents here by now. The camp was divided into a men’s and a women’s side and a portion for married couples. There was talk of removing the barriers so that men could meet new women and perhaps continue their lives. It was inevitable.

After about one-half hour of walking through the poorly lit streets between the tents, we came to the one in which Mendel thought Minski had resided. He called out a greeting and waited a moment. A hand pulled the flap back a bit and when the occupant saw Mendel, he opened and stepped back.

"Come in, Mendel," he whispered, and when the three of us stepped inside, gasped. "You, you are Herschel, the one who took the bodies from the gas building to the trench. The Sonderkommando." He screwed up his face and looked at Hans, "You, I don't remember. Were you at Kefferstadt too?"

"*Nein,*" said Hans, keeping his face in shadow. "I am a friend of Mendel and Herschel."

"Yes, Mr. Mandelbrodt, we have come to tell you that your friend Minski was murdered this morning." I watched him carefully, hoping he had already heard the news. The grapevine was rapid here in the camp.

"Yes, yes," he nodded vigorously, "I have heard. Do the guards know who did it?"

I shook my head, not wanting to tell him the news. "We think it was Granski, the Polish guard from our camp. He is here somewhere, passing himself off as a Jew."

"No, Oh *Mein Gott*. So it really was him we saw yesterday. I didn't want to believe it." He sunk down and held his head.

"Yes, we think he will kill anyone who can tell the Amis who he really is."

He looked up, his face a mask of agony, "What can we do? We must go to the Amis. Let them deal with him, the pig." He spat in the dirt floor of the tent.

"No, no, wait. We will handle this. This is an internal matter. No need to involve the Amis. Just be careful, sir." I glanced around at three other bunks, "So you are not alone here?"

Looking up at us, he said miserably, "No, there are two others who live here with me. They are in the mess tent playing at cards tonight. They will return soon."

"All right, here is what I would suggest you do. First, go to your tent mates right now. We will walk with you there. Then keep the tent well lit. Only go out in groups of two or three. I would not go even to the latrine alone, nor to the shower."

He nodded and said, "I will get myself a piece of wood, a club, like your friend here."

That is a good idea. And if you know which tent this Granski is in, please let us know. We are in number twenty-four."

Hans added, "Or let Miss Maria know in the main tent, main building now."

"Yes, also a good idea," said Mendel.

And we waited for news.

The next morning, as Hans and I were going to eat at the mess tent, a man came up and caught me by the arm, "Are you Herschel?"

"I am. Who are you?" I shook my arm free of his grip and stepped back. The man was thin, nervous, the butt of a cigarette stuck into the corner of his mouth. He had patches of graying black hair that looked like someone had grabbed handfuls and yanked it out.

"My name doesn't matter. Yoshi Mandelbrodt told me to tell you that the man you are looking for is in tent number eight seventy-five." He nodded once and was gone.

CHAPTER 25

Hans' Story

"Herschel. What will we do?" A thousand scenarios were going through my mind. Granski might be passing himself off as a camp survivor, but he was still a killer and a very frightening man.

Herschel ran his hand through his hair and said, "I don't know. Let me think."

We were still walking in the direction of the building we were working on when Chief Hawk yelled at us. "Let's get the lead out, you guys. You're burning daylight!"

We ran to the worksite. Mr. Peter Nowicki was already up on a ladder and some of our men handed long lengths of lumber up to him. I came around the end of the building and almost bumped into a group of men fashioning two ladders. A man I knew as Leib, a Romanian, was in charge of this crew. The men chiseled out notches in the long pieces and glued and nailed the crosspieces in place.

"Why are you doing it like that?" I asked frowning. It seemed a waste of time. "Why not just nail the pieces in place?"

He smiled, "Young Hans, this makes it safer, longer lasting and much stronger." He stepped back admiring the work his men were doing. "Suppose a man were climbing up high with a hod of cement or a great bundle of roof tiles, do you suppose that a couple of mere nails will hold that?"

I understood what he was saying right away, "Yes, sir, thank you for explaining. So you expect these ladders to be in use for a long time?"

He sadly shook his head. "Unfortunately, yes. Look around, my son. Each day more refugees come and no one leaves. I am afraid that we will be living in these buildings for a long time." He appraised me, "Do you expect to return to your home in the near future?"

All I could do was shake my head and mutter, "No, never."

"I, too." He slapped me on the back and helped me lift a ladder into place. "Why don't you go up onto the roof and help them nail the roof boards in place? I have heard that the Chief Hawk fellow has located a warehouse with much sheet roofing tin. If it gets here soon, we can finish this roof before nightfall."

I clambered up the ladder with my hammer stuck into my belt and encountered Herschel and two other men nailing roof boards as quickly as they were handed up. I climbed over to be next to him and again whispered, "What are we to do, Herschel? Have you thought of anything?"

"Yes," he hissed. "Tonight, after supper, I think we will pay him a visit. Maybe we can talk him into leaving the camp."

As we worked, I considered what Herschel said. I didn't think a man like Granski would succumb to our threats. After all, what did we have to threaten him with? Exposure as a former guard? Even if we exposed him, he would expose me. Then the Americans would execute us both. I did not want to die, even if it meant ensuring a man like Granski would never kill anyone again. I continued to think our best course would be to leave. But that would not keep Granski from harming someone else who might recognize him. It was a confusing problem.

At lunchtime, Miss Maria came to give us our sandwiches and some apples. "Hans," she asked, "Would you please come and help me move two desks into new offices?" She gave me a winning smile, and I saw Herschel frown.

"Oh, don't worry, Herschel, it won't take but a few moments." She led me into the main office building and into a small empty room. The light was dim and as soon as we entered, she turned and threw her arms around my neck and kissed me hungrily. I reciprocated, of course. As she pressed her warm body against mine, I realized this woman was coming to mean very much to me.

"Oh, Hans, I've missed you, I need you." She mumbled against my lips.

I pulled her tightly and buried my face in her hair. It was soft and sweet and smelled of wildflowers my sister and I'd picked for my mother. I ran my hands up her bare arms. The skin was soft and smooth as silk and it trembled under my touch. She gripped my hair in her hands and moaned softly while we just held each other. To find love in the midst of war was a very good thing, no?

"Oh, mein Gott," she moaned aloud. "I want you so badly, my Hans," but she pushed me gently away. Then she gripped my ears and pulled my face down and kissed me all over: nose, eyelids, ears cheeks and lips. "Come to me tonight. I will wait for you near the corner of this building in the shadow. Nine o'clock, yes?"

I nodded eagerly, forgetting that Herschel and I would be paying a visit of another sort this night.

We kissed long and deeply. Finally she sighed and straightened up. "Now, go back to work, my strong lad. I will think of you all day." One final kiss and I went back where my comrades were just finishing their noon meal.

Herschel asked, "I hope the desks weren't too heavy, my strong lad?" He laughed and tossed me an apple.

I grinned in embarrassment. Did he know? I looked at the other men sitting around on the pile of lumber. No one paid me the slightest attention.

Leib came over to our group and said, "A man with a truckload of roofing metal has just arrived. Herr Nowicki asked him to back up close to the other side of this building. While you men are finishing the wood, we will begin nailing the metal in place, ya?"

This sounded good to me and before anyone could say another word, I scrambled up onto the roof. Herschel followed, still chuckling and came up beside me. "Excuse me, my brother, but you have a tiny smear of something red on your neck." He touched just under my ear, and then pulled his finger away. The tip had a small smear of something red on it.

I felt my face flame and sputtered, "Must be some chalk or something."

Herschel snickered, "Must be."

In a short time we had the roof boards all on. At the other end of the building, sheets of shiny corrugated steel were being nailed in place, the grooves running from top to bottom. Our men picked their way carefully to that end, where we attempted to help.

"Nein," cried one of the men. "Too many helpers. We can do this with just the six of us." He waved his hammer, "Go, go."

I backed away a few feet, trying to see how they were installing the metal. They overlapped the corrugations two grooves and then nailed onto the ridge, not in the valley. I suppose this was to keep the rain from coming through the nail holes. The sheets were quite wide, perhaps one and one half meters, and two men were at the top putting the sheets in place and nailing them firmly. Two were at the bottom receiving the sheets from the men in the truck and handing them up. Two scrambled over the surface nailing every six or seven corrugations.

I looked at Herschel and shrugged, so we went down a ladder and looked for Chief Hawk or Mr. Nowicki or Mr. Rosen. We found Mr. Rosen arguing with a man who had clambered out of the passenger side of the truck. He was a short, well-fed burgher, with a cap on his head and nicely cut trousers and jacket. A fresh shirt gleamed under the jacket and his bulbous nose was turning crimson.

"But mein Herr, you cannot just come to my warehouse and take this roofing tin. You have to pay for it."

Rosen, exasperated, yelled, "I gave you a chit that says the U.S. Government will pay you as soon as we get our office set up here." He scratched his rear end vigorously, "That should be in a couple of weeks, like I told you."

"But I cannot eat chit. I cannot pay my bills."

Rosen leaned back, "Mister, you don't look like you've missed too many meals." He thrust the paper back in the burgher's hand and thundered, "Now get the hell out of here, you fuckin' Nazi!"

The man stiffened, nostrils flaring. He was about to utter a retort but I could see that he thought better of it. As he turned, Rosen yelled after him, "You better not clean out or lock that warehouse, or I'll have you arrested as a collaborator!"

As the truck drove off, Herschel and I stood on either side of him. Herschel said, "Thank you, Mr. Rosen."

"Ah, them fat ass so-called businessmen get my goat. It was OK for him to give his shit to the Nazis but not to us, huh?"

"Oh, I'm sure he understood you. However, I'd get a truck or two back there as soon as possible and get what you need," I replied.

"Yeah, that's probably a good idea." He looked at us and murmured, "I really couldn't have him arrested, you know. I'm just an old swabbie building some barracks with a few knuckleheads like you guys helping." He grinned at us, "Say, what are you guys doing off the roof?"

"Leib said he and his men could finish the metal roof without us, and we have completed nailing the wood boards in place. Have you got something for us to do?"

Nate Rosen looked around. "I don't. Do you see the Chief?"

Herschel and I also looked but could not see him, "No, sir

"Naw, take the rest of the day off. I'll see you back here in the morning." With that he walked off whistling.

Herschel and I walked back to our tent. I wanted to bathe and thought we should talk to Mendel and the Rabbi about what we had learned. Herschel agreed and slung his tool belt over a sweaty shoulder.

CHAPTER 26
Herschel's Story

When we arrived at the tent, Mendel and the Rabbi were nowhere to be found. Hans and I grabbed our towels and soap and headed for the nearest showers. The camp was laid out in squares with twelve large tents to a square at the upper end of each dirt street. In the lower end the tents were smaller. I supposed they thought there would not be this many people here. I estimated there were more than one hundred squares now.

There were two main streets laid out in a north-south direction and cross streets every two squares. The streets had signs with numbers for the cross streets and A and B for the main streets. Each wooden road sign had numerous smaller signs, most hand lettered in Hebrew, Polish, Hungarian and any number of other languages indicating dining tents, latrines, shower tents and areas where the men could play games of football, cards, chess, singing, and the like. Many groups had formed as the camp grew. There were even theatrical performances in the dining tents each evening. Somehow, musical instruments had been fabricated or procured and frequently the strains of a melancholy violin or clarinet could be heard. The strumming of a guitar or mandolin often echoed between these fabric shelters. Was life returning to normal or were men just attempting to stave off the darkness in their hearts?

As the tent squares were replaced with buildings, each would receive a name from its occupants. Right now, each tent had a large white numeral painted on the front of it. The newer tents held twelve or more while our tents were just for four. I noticed that there were still some four-man tents scattered in the squares. I don't believe the planners ever thought that the camps would be as large as they were, and they were still growing.

Every four squares had a wash tent with six showers. Each morning, water trucks supplied the overhead tanks in the center of the wash tents. There were now two large dining tents, and Chief Hawk told the men more workers would soon be required as orders came down to replace the dining tents with buildings ASAP, whatever that meant.

Across the road was the camp for the former guards and behind our camp was the women's camp. It was rumored that the fence separating our camp from the women's would be removed shortly. Married men were permitted to visit their wives and children and even stay the night, but single men were strongly urged to stay away, at least for the present. Each day, however, one could see men and women at the fence talking, exchanging food or small gifts. The Americans saw no reason to keep the camps separated any longer. I think they did it so that individuals could regain some weight, receive appropriate medical attention and perhaps come to terms with their grief. I do not know. I am not a psychologist.

The war had been over now for several months. Hitler was declared dead, though no soldier from the Allied forces could claim to have seen his body. The Russians reported that they had charge of the body and that of his mistress, Eva Braun. Many in the high command had been taken into custody or had disappeared. There were rumors of a war crimes trial but no one knew where or when it would take place.

There were also rumors that the Nazis had killed four million, then six million then eight million Jews, Polish and Russian prisoners, political enemies, Gypsies, the aged, the crippled, dwarves, even twins. Daily the rumors swirled and if one believed even half to be true, it was a global disaster of epic proportions.

When we returned to the tent, Reb Horowitz and Mendel were playing chess on a small table outside. We threw our towels over a line and slipped into clean clothes, before joining them.

The Rabbi turned his head and smiled, "Good afternoon, boys. A little early to stop for the day?"

I explained why we'd finished early and then told them about Granski and that Hans and I planned to pay him a visit that night to urge him in the strongest possible terms that he leave the camp.

"I don't think that is a very good idea. What if he is armed? What if he, shall we say, doesn't take kindly to your suggestion?" The Rabbi was very earnest and leaned forward, forearms resting on his knees, the chess game forgotten.

"Let me get some more men, and we will all go. Maybe he will listen if there is a crowd," insisted Mendel.

"No, no," Hans cried in alarm, "we cannot do that. If he points me out and the men believe him, then they will kill me too."

"Yes, I see," said Mendel thoughtfully. "So what will we do?"

"We? We? There is no 'we', Mendel. You stay here with the Rabbi. This is for Hans and me to take care of."

"I am coming with you," insisted Mendel. "I need to see this Granski you are so afraid of."

"No, Mendel, he is a very dangerous man," emphasized Hans. "I saw him shoot three men to death."

"And he would have shot me if Hans hadn't stepped between us," I declared.

"All right, I will still go with you, but I will stay behind, out of sight, when you confront him. I just want to get a look at him."

"Boys, I implore you, please do not do this. Just tell the American soldiers. Let them take care of him," urged the Rabbi.

"Sir, you know we cannot do that. If we can get him to leave the camp, I will be safe. Please, Rabbi, try to look at this from our standpoint."

"Yes, sir, you know my reasons. Please understand," urged Hans.

"But suppose he won't go? How far are you willing to go in, uh, urging him?"

Hans stiffened, "If we have to, we will kill him. He is an evil man."

Now it was my turn to be taken aback. "Hans, you never said anything about killing him. I don't know if..."

He rounded on me, "Herschel, I am not going back to that camp. If you don't have the heart for this, then stay here. I will go alone. He has already killed one more of us. How many more does he have to kill for us to take action?"

"No!" insisted the Rabbi, standing and pointing at Hans. "No, I will not allow you to kill him!" He gripped Hans by the upper arm and put his face close. "No, no, no. Up to now, have you ever killed a man?"

Hans tried to pull his arm free. "No, sir, I have never killed anyone, but I am not going back to that prison camp. If I have to kill that piece of dung, I will, and have no ill dreams later."

"I am sorry, my son, but that just makes you as bad a man as he. Don't you see?" His face was a mask of agony, tears forming in the corners of his eyes.

"Rabbi," I begged, "we are just going to talk to him, warn him. However, if he attacks us, we will defend ourselves. But only then, all right? Hans?"

Reluctantly Hans nodded.

We went to eat, the four of us.

Later that evening, I took up my hammer and Hans retrieved his wooden cudgel. As we walked out of the tent, Mendel behind us, I looked back. In the glow of the tent lantern, I saw the Rabbi standing, hands pressed to his eyes. His shoulders were shaking. After all we'd been through, after all the death we both had seen, for us to kill one man, a very bad man, disturbed him so much. I was stunned to my core, so much that I had to stop and steady myself.

"What is wrong, Herschel?" asked Hans, concerned. He put an arm around my shoulders to steady me.

Mendel came up and also put an arm around my waist. "Are you ill, Herschel?"

I shook my head, stopped and stifled my own sob. I looked at each of them and nodded toward our tent and just said, "The Rabbi."

They looked, and Mendel gasped, "What have we done?"

"Nothing," said Hans quietly, "It's what we may do."

I struggled to my feet, "Come, we must just talk to Granski, and then we must get back to the Rabbi."

They nodded and we set off up "A" Street to look for tent number 875. We passed many men sitting outside the tents on this a pleasant late spring evening. Several greeted Mendel and me. At the junction of a cross street, Mendel stopped by a group of three men. They greeted him with ribald jests and he grinned as he slapped a slim, balding man on the back.

"Ho, Gad, can you tell us where we can find tent number 875?"

The men fell silent and Gad took a step away. "875? Why that one, Mendel?"

Taken aback, Mendel could only say, "Why, we just wish to talk to one of the men in that tent."

Gad looked around uneasily, "There is only one man in that tent." He looked at the three of us, then at our tools, my hammer and Hans' wooden club.

Puzzled, I asked, "Are these tents meant for more than one?"

Another of the men said, "There were four of them but three moved out. They said it was, um, uncomfortable." He pointed up the road, "875 is three streets up. Good luck." The three men turned and shuffled away.

"Come," I said motioning the others. We walked up the darkening street until we made out the number 875 on canvas at a corner, next to a shower tent.

Hans pushed aside the flap. It was dark inside. We crowded the opening. "No one here," I said scanning what I could see.

I heard a strangled cry behind me. Hans fell against me and I staggered into the tent. I turned just in time to see Granski standing over Mendel, a knife in his hand, blood covering the blade.

Hans clutched his upper arm. He swung the club at Granski's head, but Granski just dodged the blow and laughed.

"You fools, you think to take me unaware?" He nudged Mendel with his booted foot, "And you bring this cripple? Pahh," he spat at my feet. "I should kill you both." He stepped towards me, and I lashed out with my foot, hitting him behind the leg.

He grunted and went down on a knee. Before I could draw back, he jabbed the bloody knife into my calf.

I screamed in pain and saw Hans loom over us, but Granski must have sensed him also. He swung a fist back and caught Hans in the stomach. Hans fell back and I tried to get to my feet. The knife lashed out again and tore through Hans' bicep. The blood immediately soaked his shirtsleeve and dripped on me.

A voice called out, "Vas? Vas is los?" We heard the sound of several footsteps in the gravel, and Granski was gone.

I crawled to Hans, who was wrapping a handkerchief around his upper arm.

"Are you hurt, Herschel?" he asked.

"My leg. It is cut. That bastard, he cut us both." I looked at where the men were kneeling and struggled to my feet. I held out a hand and Hans came to stand beside me. We hurried to the men and I pushed one aside. Mendel lay on his back while blood soaked into the ground around his head. I cradled his head in my arms and saw that he was still alive, though barely. In the dim light of a lantern held by one of the men, I saw his pale skin and the thin red line under his chin. His eyes fluttered, and he tried to speak.

We leaned close and all he said was, "Yisroel." His eyes looked directly at me, and the life went out of them.

I stifled a sob, and Hans gripped my shoulder. I sat rocking poor Mendel and vowed I would avenge him, no matter what the Rabbi said. It was now very personal. In a few minutes, two soldiers ran up and pulled me away from Mendel. I tried talking to them, and several men were also gesticulating and shouting that it was not me, that it was the man who lived in the tent. In the confusion, I looked for Hans but he was gone.

One of the soldiers left and in a few minutes came back with several more, two with a stretcher and another wore an armband with a red cross on it. He checked Mendel for pulse and breath then shook his head. The men holding the stretcher unfolded a sheet, wrapped Mendel in it and carefully lifted our comrade onto the stretcher.

A soldier questioned some of the men but I could tell that this would be just a cursory investigation. In the land of death, at the end of a horrible war, what was another death?

Now I had to find Granski - and Hans.

CHAPTER 27
Hans' Story

I could do nothing for my friend, Mendel, and the last thing I wanted was to be held by the American soldiers. The dark concealed me as I made my way back to our tent and the Rabbi.

He was sitting where we'd left him, his head nodding, lips moving soundlessly, eyes closed. I sat next to him and he appeared to sense my presence, but didn't stop. I listened carefully, he was mumbling in Hebrew. A prayer?

Reb Horowitz stopped and opened his eyes. The old man looked twenty years older than when we'd left. I placed a hand on his leg and told him about Mendel, how Granski had ambushed us and stabbed Herschel and me. With that, I remembered my arm.

He gave a cry, covered his eyes and sobbed.

"Reb Horowitz, sir, will you help me, please?" I unwrapped the rag from my bicep.

With a sigh, the Rabbi struggled to his feet, gripping my shoulder. "Come into the light, my son." He then asked, "Who is tending to poor Mendel?"

"Herschel was still there when I left. He was holding him. I couldn't stay. The soldiers were coming."

We went into the tent, and I sat on my bunk while the Rabbi turned up the lamp and held it close. "I think this should be sewn together, Hans. I will get my sewing kit." He cocked an eye at me, "I don't believe you want to go to the medical clinic?"

"No, sir. Please do what you have to do."

He produced a small bottle of vodka that Mendel had somehow procured. "Here, pour some of this on your wound. It will burn, but it will cleanse. Save some for the thread." He came near with a needle and some white thread. Before sewing, he passed the tip of the needle through the flame in the lamp and dipped the thread in the vodka.

I removed my bloody shirt and wiped the blood off my arm, then splashed some vodka on the open wound. The sharp pain made me gasp and I gripped the arm of the chair tightly. With a few quick strokes the Rabbi slid the needle through the flesh, pulling the loose edges together. I moaned through my gritted teeth.

The stitches were even and carefully knotted. "Rabbi, how did you know what to do?"

"How?" he snorted, "I am a rabbi. Would you like a circumcision next?"

Now I chuckled through the pain, "Too late, old man. My father had me done as a babe."

"Good. It will be easier to pass you off as a Jew." He finished up and inspected his work. "You will have a nice scar, my boy. Tell them it is from dueling. The

ladies will love it." He sighed as he put his tools away. Then he turned and wrapped a clean handkerchief around the wound. "What will you do now? Where is Granski?"

"I do not know but Herschel and I will find him and avenge Mendel."

The Rabbi stood suddenly, towering over me, "Have you learned nothing, you foolish boy?" He leaned his face close to mine, "I forbid you to pursue this man. He will only kill the two of you!" Striding back and forth in the small tent, he whirled on me, "What has become of Mendel? We must take care of the boy's body" His voice was shaking.

Stubbornly I glared back at him, "Yes, yes, we will. Granski killed Mendel! Not I. Not Herschel! Do you understand?" I took a drink of the vodka. It tasted foul and I spat it on the floor at his feet. " He stabbed Herschel and killed my friend! I will not rest until that man is dead! We...."

Just them Herschel entered the tent, limping.

Both the Rabbi and I wrapped our arms around him and helped him to his bed. "Herschel, have you had your leg taken care of?" I asked while the Rabbi pulled his trouser leg up. The bandage covered from his ankle almost to his knee.

"Yes, the medics took me to the first aid tent and sewed me up. How is your arm, Hans?"

I showed him the white cloth Rabbi Horowitz had tied over the stitched wound. "A first rate job. This man is a genius. He saved my life." Remembering how sad the Rabbi looked when we left, I felt, perhaps, some praise would cheer him up.

He glared at me and said, "Saved your life? Ten of you are not worth one Mendel!" He stood and stormed out of the tent.

Herschel and I sat and looked guiltily at each other. "You know it is my fault that Mendel is dead. We must find Granski and kill him for what he did." My resolve was made of steel. I would not rest until I ripped that dog apart.

"Yes, yes, but let us get some rest now. My leg is throbbing, and I'm sure your arm is not any better." He glanced at the doorway, "Let the old man fume for tonight. Tomorrow, after work, we will search for Granski. Perhaps Miss Maria can help."

I smacked my forehead, "Maria!" I just remembered that we were supposed to meet. I looked at the small clock that sat on the Rabbi's side table. Near midnight. Too late. I hoped that she had not waited too long. I would explain everything to her tomorrow. Little did I know that this night was not yet over.

CHAPTER 28
Herschel's Story

It seemed like we were not alone for long when we awoke to much noise outside the tent. I swung my legs over the edge of the bed with a gasp of pain, when the tent flap was pulled open. There were two American soldiers on either side of the opening, and an officer strode in. He had an electric torch in his hand and shined it in my face.

"You two boys Herschel and Hans Rothberg?" he asked abruptly.

I held my hand in front of my eyes. "Yes sir. Is there a problem?" I tried not to look at Hans. I noted that the Rabbi's bunk was empty so, of course, was Mendel's.

"You guys want to come with me? Do you know a Rabbi Horowitz? Maria, works in Admin, says he bunks with you. That right?"

"Yes, that is correct. Is he all right?" I was up and carefully pulled my trousers on over my bandages and slid my feet into my shoes. Hans was also dressing quickly.

"Oh, he's okay, just making a nuisance of himself. He's in the morgue tent with some guy named Mendel we brought in earlier. Got knifed in a scuffle. This Rabbi Horowitz told the doc some cock and bull story about how the guy who killed this Mendel was a former guard in a concentration camp who was passing himself off as a Jew." He eyed us squinting in the bright beam. "You know anything about that?"

Before Hans could say anything, I said, "We heard rumors, the same as you, sir, but that is all."

He looked at us, frowning, "Say, how did you get those wounds? What's under those bandages?"

"I received mine this evening from the same man who killed our friend Mendel. You can ask the doctor at the first aid tent. I was taken there earlier tonight." I had to think fast. "My brother received his today working for Chief Hawk on the roof of the new building. We were passing up some metal roofing and one slipped." I shrugged, "Small cuts and abrasions are quite common when doing construction work, sir. You can ask the Chief."

He seemed to accept this explanation. "Okay. Well, c'mon and get your Rabbi Horowitz." He spun around and strode out of the tent. The two soldiers waited for us, their rifles held at port arms.

We followed as best we could, me limping and Hans helping, and soon came to an illuminated tent with a bright red cross on a field of white painted on it. The officer held the flap back, and Hans and I entered. We heard mumbling and followed the sound. The tent was divided into several sections by canvas attached to metal poles. We moved toward the rear, and a female nurse bade us to come in.

The Rabbi sat slumped in a wooden chair next to the metal table that held Mendel's body. It was covered with a sheet from his neck down. The Rabbi held a limp, pale hand and pressed it to his forehead. He was saying the Kaddish, the Hebrew prayer for the dead, over and over. "Yisgadel V'yiskadesh shmeh rabboh!"

He was weeping. We went and stood on either side of him. Gently I said, "You know, you are only supposed to say this with a minyan, Rabbi." We lifted him by the arms and I smiled at him and assured him that tomorrow we would gather the requisite ten men. "After all, Mendel was a well-liked and respected young man."

We steered the dazed man past the guards and took him back to our lonely tent. "Get some sleep, Reb Horowitz. Tomorrow we will hold a service for Mendel."

Though I was exhausted, I could not get to sleep. I kept picturing Mendel on that table. He looked to be sleeping peacefully. But I wasn't peaceful. That evil Granski was responsible and he would die. I promised myself, and Mendel's spirit, that I would see to it. Tomorrow would be a busy day.

The morning came with fog and a drizzle of rain. A cloud of sadness seemed to hang over the camp. We silently dressed, Hans and I. The Rabbi had slept in his clothes.

As we were preparing to leave, the Rabbi put up an arm, "Wait, my sons. I have something to say to you."

I sighed. Were we going to get more of his admonitions of peace and brotherhood? More of how Mendel was worth more than all of us put together?

Hans and I sat on my bunk, and I'm sure he was thinking the same thing.

The Rabbi sat up facing us and said, "My boys, I am truly sorry for my harsh words last night. Mendel was a good boy, but so are you two. You are my sons, all three of you. Please forgive me for being an old fool. I was angry and that foul man, Granski, should suffer my words, not you."

We stood and went to him. I kissed his gaunt face on both cheeks and took one of his hands in mine, as did Hans. "Of course, sir. You are our friend. We would forgive you anything."

"Yes, sir. You have made us better men," Hans stated.

"Good, good," he mumbled. "Now let us eat and then take care of Mendel."

We met the Chief and the rest of the work crew in the mess tent.

"I heard about your friend Mendel," said the Chief. "Sorry. Why don't you fellas take the day off?"

"Thank you, sir," answered Hans. "We are going to hold a service for him. We will be at work later. I think we need to work to take our mind off what happened."

"I understand," he replied. "Come on over whenever you're ready, O.K.?" He turned and held his hand out to the Rabbi. "I'm sorry, sir."

Petty Officers Rosen and Nowicki each shook our hands, mumbling their condolences. We thanked them with a nod. Then they followed the Chief out into the mist.

After breakfast, the Reb stood on a chair and clapped his hands for order. "My friends, please!" After the talk and the shushing had died away, he announced,

"For those of you who have not heard, our young friend, Mendel, was killed last night."

Shouts of, "No!" and "Mein Gott!" were shouted numerous times. A voice called out, "Who did this foul deed?" And another, "Was it an accident?"

The Rabbi clapped again, harder this time, "Nein, he was murdered by a man named Granski. A man who was a Nazi guard at our camp; a man who is passing himself off as a Jew. He slept in tent number 875. If any of you see him or know him, please tell the American soldiers. Let them deal with him, please." Before he stepped down, he looked at Hans and mouthed the words, "I'm sorry."

Hans just nodded.

"We are going to have a short service here for our young friend. If you knew him or would just like to pay your respects, please stay after you are finished eating." With that, he stepped down and sat to resume meditating.

We stayed for the sad Kaddish, as did more than two hundred men. Several told stories from when he first arrived at this camp, some funny, some heartbreaking. No one had a disparaging word for our friend. By the end of the service, many of these hardened men were openly weeping. These men who had seen death a thousand times over, some men like myself, Sonderkommando, those whose job it had been to gather the clothes and valuables, to extract the gold teeth, to pile and move the corpses of men, women and children, wept for one good man. That he should have survived that life in the death camp only to be killed in a DP camp, where he thought he would be safe, was a tragedy.

Hans and I vowed never to be alone and never to let the Rabbi go out alone until Granski was dead or locked up by the Americans.

A short time after walking the Rabbi back to our tent and making sure a friend, Ari Griek, stayed with him, Hans and I went back to our building.

It was almost completed. We were putting up the interior dividing walls, and Mr. Rosen was showing us how to string electrical wire to outlets. We worked to near exhaustion to keep busy. As the day came to a close we excused ourselves and went back toward our tent.

On the way, Maria stepped out from the main tent, "I heard, Hans, Herschel." She gripped both of our hands, "I'm so, so sorry." She looked imploringly at Hans.

He turned to me, "Go on. I will return in a few minutes, Herschel."

I nodded, understanding that they wanted a few minutes together.

When I came in, Ari nodded his balding head and left.

"So, Rabbi, anything exciting happen today?" I asked while pulling my shirt over my head.

He smiled wanly, "No, young man, I have just been reading the Talmud. Was everything well with you?"

"Yes, sir," I said. "We have almost finished the office building. I reached for my towel and sighed tiredly, "Come, Reb, let us go to the shower tent. A nice hot shower will do us both good."

He agreed and also picked up his towel. "Please let me borrow that pocket knife you have, my son. I need to trim my toenails."

We strolled the quiet streets, nodding occasionally to an acquaintance. Most of the men were at dinner or sitting in clusters outside the mess tent. The Reb stopped for a minute to chat with an older man.

As I entered the shower tent, I saw that I was alone. I hung our towels over the rope that divided the stalls and folded my clothes onto a bench that stood outside each shower enclosure. I laughed; did these Americans never take baths?

Just as I stepped naked onto the slatted floor under a nozzle, I heard footsteps and realized another was present. Before I could turn, I was slammed on the side of my head and everything swam before my eyes. Another blow to my stomach took all my breath. I fell to one knee, trying to look up at what happened. A third blow knocked me onto my stomach. I managed to roll on my back and look up.

It was Granski. He held a knife, and was laughing, "Jew, did you think I had run away? Did you think I would forget you? You and that Private Rothberg? I will finally finish you, then that old fool Rabbi, and the traitor." He stepped menacingly toward me, and I could do nothing.

So this is how it was going to end? In a shower stall in a DP camp? It was not much different from the gas building. Those people were told that they were just going to get a shower and delousing before assigned to work teams. They died in the 'shower rooms', as would I.

Just as Granski raised his knife to plunge into my exposed chest, I heard a shriek. The Rabbi had come in and seen what was about to happen. He had my knife unclasped and he leaped for Granski. The former guard took the full weight of the Rabbi on his back, but he didn't go down. He tried to reach over his shoulder, but the Rabbi had clasped his legs around Granski's waist. As he squeezed, he tried to avoid the hands that reached for him.

Granski was flailing with his knife and the Rabbi was getting cut on his arm, which was around Granski's throat. With another shriek, Reb Horowitz, a man of God, an Orthodox rabbi, a peaceful man, plunged his knife into Granski's chest.

I saw all this from the floor where I was attempting to regain my breath. The Rabbi was a wild man. He bit Granski's ear and would not let go. Again and again the knife fell, shredding Granski's shirt and chest. Great splashes of blood flew in all directions, splattering me and the curtains of the stalls.

Still Granski didn't drop. He staggered, trying to dislodge the crazed man on his back. With a muffled grunt he reached over his shoulder and grabbed the Rabbi's hair and pulled.

One of the Rabbi's wild slashes carved out a deep wound to Granski's throat cutting the carotid artery. The blood spouted and Granski went down on one knee. A second stab, just missing his own arm, dropped Granski. He finally fell face first beside me, the knife dropping free of his lifeless hand.

I kicked it away and struggled to my knees to stop the Rabbi, who was now stabbing Granski in the back, grunting each time. I put a hand out to catch his arm and he looked at me with wild hatred in his eyes. He was completely crazed.

"Rabbi, stop, it is me, Herschel. Stop. He is dead."

One final time, he plunged my knife up to its hilt in Granski's back and seemed to come back to reality. He looked down at the knife and the blood seeping from the wound on his own arm. With a cry, Reb Horowitz jumped up with a hand over his mouth. "My God, what have I done?" He couldn't tear his eyes away from the knife sticking out from between Granski's shoulders. I crawled over and pulled the knife free. I quickly wiped it on Granski's shredded shirt.

As I struggled to my feet, I went to him, trying to insert myself between the old man and Granski's bloody corpse. I touched his arm and he looked down at my hand as if he'd never seen it. Slowly he raised his eyes to mine. His look was blank, without any emotion. He raised his hand and took mine off his arm and pushed it down to my side. Then he turned and walked out of the tent. I hurriedly washed the blood from my face and chest.

I gathered my wits, dressed, stuffed the knife in my pocket, then stepped outside. A man I recognized was walking by. I raised a hand to stop him. "Mr. Levine, would you please get the American soldiers? There is a dead man in here."

He stopped in his tracks, "What did you say? Is anyone else hurt?"

Mr. Levine was a short, stocky man I knew was from Birkenau, a survivor. "No, no one else hurt. I just came in and found him. Please hurry," I implored.

Just then two men came up with towels around their necks. "Please, gentlemen, I just found a man dead in here. Could you wait or go to another shower?"

Looking astonished, the men hurried away. I don't know how long it took but several soldiers came trotting up the street, followed by the same officer who had come to us the previous evening.

He brushed past me and entered the shower tent. I heard an intake of breath, then he came out and stood in the growing dusk with me. He lit a cigarette and inhaled deeply.

"You know the dead guy, kid?"

I nodded. "He is the man who killed my friend Mendel, the one the Rabbi was with last night."

He just nodded. "You kill him?" Now he turned his head and looked at me.

I shook my head wearily, "No, sir, I found him like this. It is good he is dead. He was a bad man, a former guard from our camp."

"So that wasn't a made up story?"

"No. He probably thought he was far enough away and would not get caught. I guess he did not think others, survivors from our camp, would be here." I shook my head again. "He also killed a man last week who was from our camp." Again I repeated, "It is good he is dead. The war is over. Perhaps now we may live in peace."

The officer snorted, "It's over here, but the war is still going on in the Pacific. Do you think it will ever end?"

I shrugged, "It seems like there will always be war somewhere. I, myself, am so tired of it all. Are you not sick of it all, too?"

"You bet, kid." He ground the butt out on the ground and said, "Go on home and get some sleep. I know where to find you if I need you."

"Thank you, sir." I walked back down the street, forgetting the towels in the shower room. We could draw more tomorrow.

CHAPTER 29
Hans' Story

Maria pulled me into the unfinished building and deep into a shadowed corner. I pulled her close and she rested her head on my shoulder, her arms around my waist. "Oh, my love, I feel so bad about poor Mendel. I liked him so much. Everyone did."

"Ya, he was a good friend. Herschel and I will find the man who did this and finish him."

She pulled back and looked into my face. "You don't mean kill him, do you?"

"Of course I do. He was a bad man before and is a worse man now. He deserves to die."

"Oh, Hans, don't say that. It is not for you to be judge, jury and executioner. Let the American Army take care of him. They are already keeping all the former camp guards in their own prison across the road." Her voice dropped, "I have heard that they intend to try them by a military tribunal and hang them."

I gulped. If she only know who she was talking to. I kissed her once to hide my nervousness and said, "I must get back to the Rabbi and Herschel. I cannot leave them alone. This madman may come after them too."

"Yes, all right, my Hans. I understand. Will you come to work in the morning?"

"Of course. They need me. Herschel too. They cannot construct this building without the Rothberg brothers!" Each day it seemed more comfortable saying and even believing this.

A quick last kiss and we walked back into the twilight. Up ahead I saw a squad of soldiers marching quickly up the street. "Goodnight, Maria. I will see you tomorrow after breakfast."

She smiled and said, "Until the morning, Hans." Then she walked around a corner of the building and was gone.

I was dirty and sweaty and wanted nothing more than to take a bath or, rather, a shower, as the American and the UNRRC people had not seen fit to install bathing tubs for us.

The tent seemed empty, but I could make out the Rabbi, who lay curled into a fetal position in the dark corner of his bunk. I went and gently shook his shoulder, "Rabbi, Rabbi, are you awake?"

He slowly rolled over, and I gasped when I saw the blood on his clothes. "What happened? Are you hurt?" I could hardly believe my eyes but when I reached for his shirt, he put out a hand.

"No, young man, I am not injured, at least not physically. I have committed a terrible sin." Then he slowly and almost inaudibly told me all that had happened that evening.

The practical side of me took over. "Reb, stand up. Remove your clothes and give them to me." I reached into his trunk and gave him a clean shirt and trousers. "Quickly. The soldiers may come at any moment."

He stood and then sat again, unsure what to do, attempting to hurry. When he had his trousers in hand, I wiped his hands and throat with a damp cloth. Then I bundled the blood-soaked clothes tightly and left the tent. The nearest refuse bin was just one street over, but I hurried to the building site and placed them in a large steel trash container, covering them with building scraps.

When I returned, Herschel was sitting with the Rabbi. He held the old man's hand and bent his head closely. The Rabbi was shaking his head from side to side, sitting in his underclothes, his skinny frame looking weak, his face sallow.

"No, no, no, Herschel. God will never forgive me for taking a life."

"But you saved my life!"

"No, not I. That was a madman who took control of my body." He gripped his hair and made to tear it out, but he lacked the strength. "Oy, what will I do?"

His agony was pathetic. What could we do? It was over, done with. Granski, the monster, was dead.

Herschel stood up and pointed a finger at the old man. He was nearly enraged at this point. "Stop it! Just stop it! You feel sorry for yourself? Good. If it will make you sad to feel sorry for taking the life of that ball of dung, then do so, but you did it so I would live. And for that, I thank you." He leaned over the Rabbi, who sat rocking back and forth, his thin arms crossed over his chest. "Don't you even try to make me feel bad."

Herschel turned and spat on the floor. "You self-righteous old fool, we worked taking the bodies out of the gas building. We were part of the killing machine! We were Sonderkommandos."

The Rabbi leaped up, his face a mask of total agony, "No, don't say that. Until this night, I have never killed anyone!"

I snorted, "I would kill that man a hundred times and not feel one pang of guilt. You did what had to be done."

The Rabbi looked from one to the other of us wildly, "Mein Gott, what has happened? What will become of us?"

I did not know what to make of this. "At least finish putting your clothes on, old man," I said gently, attempting to help him.

The Rabbi slapped my hands away. He was visibly shaking. With a last look at us, he screeched, "I need some time alone!" He grabbed his clothes and rushed from the tent.

Herschel plunked himself down on his bunk, deflated. "Perhaps we should go after him?"

I shrugged dismissively, "No, let him be for a while. He will come to his senses once he has time to think about it. I think we need some quiet time too."

Herschel walked me up to our nearby shower tent. The soldiers had removed the body and scrubbed down the floor to rid it of blood. Faint traces could still be seen on the wooden floor.

I showered quickly, the room making me very uncomfortable. At last, Granski was dead. Neither Herschel nor I had killed him, and I was now safe. I doubted if I would ever come upon Commandant Boettcher or if he would remember me. As far as I was concerned, the long, terrible war was ended, and I now wished to continue my life, perhaps with Maria and Herschel. He was truly my brother.

Neither of us was hungry that evening so we sat and played cards and then took a walk. We greeted friends and received many condolences for Mendel. When it was time for bed, the Rabbi had still not returned. "Should we go look for him?" I asked Herschel.

"I do not think so. He must understand and accept what has happened. Just wait, you will see, by morning life will go on and he will be lecturing in the mess tent." He disrobed and climbed into his bunk.

"If he comes in during the night and I hear him, I will wake you, yes?"

"Yes, yes, fine."

"Herschel?"

"Yes, Hans?"

"Do you think God forgives?"

He barked a short laugh, "God? There is no God, Hans."

"But he is all powerful, all forgiving. That's what we were taught in church."

"All powerful? Hah! If He were all-powerful, would He have let happen what did happen over the last eight or ten years? No, my friend, my brother, if God is good, and the Devil is evil, then for the past years the Devil has been winning. In the last war, he won also. I am afraid if God exists, he has taken a back seat- if you believe in that sort of religious shit. I do not any longer." Herschel rolled over and went to sleep.

The next morning, we were surprised that the Rabbi had still not returned. At breakfast in the mess tent, we still had not found him. "He probably spent the night walking about or with some friends. He will turn up when he gets hungry," I said. Herschel and I were very hungry and went back to the serving tables two times. Then we each pocketed an apple and went to find Chief Hawk.

The Chief stood in front of the nearly finished building, Nowicki and Rosen stood behind him. He looked somber. "I was just about to send someone to find you two.

CHAPTER 30
Herschel's Story

The Chief looked somber, as did Mr. Nowicki and Mr. Rosen. Behind them, Sam Katz and the other men were just standing and watching us. Out of the corner of my eye, I saw Miss Maria standing by the corner of our building.

There was definitely something odd going on. I looked from one to the other of the men. "What is wrong, Chief Hawk?"

"Would you boys please come over here and sit down for a coupla minutes?" He indicated a bench against the side of one wall. The Chief withdrew a green pack of cigarettes from his shirt pockets, shook one out and lit it with his large silver lighter.

Hans and I sat on either side of him. The rain from the previous day had stopped, and the clouds had cleared. I took a deep breath and inhaled the smell of fresh wood, cement and odors from the cook tent. It felt like life was returning to normal. I frowned at the Chief. "What do you need, sir?"

"When did you last see your friend, the Rabbi?"

Hans perked up, an anxious look on his face. "Last evening, sir. We talked for a bit, and then he went for a walk. Herschel and I played cards for, perhaps one hour, then went to bed. Why? Have you seen him?"

"Yes, I'm afraid we have." He stood. "Come with me.

I looked worriedly at Hans, and then we followed the Chief. He led us into the unfinished end of the building. He hesitated before opening an inside door. In the room that opened was a shadow. I craned my neck to see past the Chief. As he opened the door fully, some light spilled in.

Beside me, Hans gasped. Hanging from a ceiling joist was a figure. It was, as I had feared, the Rabbi. His feet were off the floor, a toppled wooden crate next to them. His hands hung loosely by his side and, though he had strangled horribly, a faint smile was on his haggard face. Around his neck was a length of electric wire. It had cut deeply into his meager flesh. His head was unnaturally tilted to one side.

Hans was softly sobbing. Quietly, so only I could hear him, he said, "Herschel, what have we done?"

I could only shake my head. What had we done? We didn't do this, he did. The Rabbi had killed himself. Was I to blame? He stabbed Granski, thus saving my life. Did that make me responsible? No, I refused to feel it was my fault. I did not bring Granski to this camp. I wanted to reason with him. I wanted him to leave. No, he chose to stay and begin killing men from Kefferstadt. If the Rabbi hadn't stopped him, I would be dead right now. No doubt, he would have eliminated the Rabbi and Hans and who knows how many others? I wanted the Rabbi to be alive so I could tell him this again and again. I couldn't cry. I tried but couldn't force the tears. I was inured to death. It had no meaning any longer. For more years than I could count, I had been immersed in it. After you've cleared a gas building and piled corpses of men, women and even children on a flat, wheeled trolley, the color of dung, towed it to a gash in the earth and dumped the corpses in, does the death of one more man even have meaning?

The Rabbi and Mendel had been my friends but now they were dead. I was still alive. It was my duty to go on. It was my solemn, holy duty to live a life that would honor them. But was it my duty to have children and, once again, produce more of the Jewish race for another so-called master race to annihilate? Never, ever again would a Jew wait in fear for that midnight tread outside his door and go meekly away to the gas buildings and the ovens. I swore in my heart to Mendel, to the Rabbi and to the millions who'd perished that this Jew would fight to his last breath before someone in power would march me off that way.

I turned to the Chief, "Cut him down please."

Chief Hawk shook his head, "Can't yet. The doc and soldiers have to declare him dead first."

I slowly rounded on him, fists clenched, "Cut him down, goddammit! He is dead!" I shouted. "He deserves better than that!" I moved to the Rabbi's corpse and grabbed his legs and tried to lift him. "Help me. Please, help me!"

Hans came up to me and gripped me around the waist, pulling me back. I held on, then let my arms drop. My face was wet and I wiped it with my shirtsleeve. Was it raining in here? Did I have something in my eye?

The room was suddenly full of men. One soldier stood on the crate and felt the Rabbi's neck for a pulse. When he couldn't detect one, he signaled two of the other soldiers, and they lifted the body until he could unwind the wire. They laid the body on a stretcher and covered it with a blanket.

"I'm Captain Evans. I'm the doctor here at the camp." He shook the Chief's hand and then nodded at Hans and me. He indicated the now empty electric cord hanging from the beam, "Anybody know him?"

I stepped forward and opened my mouth, but the Chief motioned me back. He said to Dr. Evans, "Yeah, he's been around here a couple of times. His name is, was, Rabbi Horowitz. I don't know what his first name was."

"A Jew, huh? Camp survivor?" Asked the doctor, not looking anymore at Hans or me.

"Uh-huh,"

"Yeah, well, he's not the first. Probably won't be the last." He made a note on a card he took from his shirt pocket. "You Seabees, Chief?"

"Yep. This is my building. Be done in another coupla days." He shook a cigarette from the pack and offered one to the doc. "You know what we're doin' next?"

The doc shook his head, "No. What?" He took the cigarette and waited for the Chief to flick open his lighter, then leaned forward and sucked in the smoke.

Chief Hawk smiled. "Medical center. Sickbay. I don't know, what do you guys call it?"

"Field Hospital." The doc had a hopeful look on his face. Then he straightened his hat, cleared his throat and looked the Chief in the eye. "You want us to bury him?"

Chief Hawk glared over the doc's shoulder at us. "I'll send somebody around to collect him tomorrow morning, O.K.? We'll take him out back and bury him."

"Sounds good. I've got better things for my guys to do." He shook the Chief's hand again and said, "Sign here and I'll see you when you start the Field Hospital." He turned on his heel and left.

"Why did you stop us from talking about the Rabbi?" I asked. I was curious. It couldn't have been in deference to the Rabbi. The Chief barely knew him.

Chief Hawk motioned us back outside, and we again sat on the wooden bench. He smoked in silence. I noticed that Mr. Nowicki and Mr. Rosen had put the men back to work. We sat while all around us there were men lifting, carrying, hammering and measuring.

"There will most likely be an investigation once word gets out about the Rabbi." He turned to us and said, "I've been talking to Petty Officer Nowicki to get you boys sponsored for immigration to the United States. To Chicago. Nowicki's family runs a contracting business in Chicago, and it looks like they will do it for him." He took a last puff on the cigarette, then crushed the tip out on the edge of the bench, ripped it open and scattered the remaining ash and tobacco on the ground. Then he balled up the bit of paper and stuck it in a pocket of his pressed khaki trousers.

"If you get caught up in the investigation, it might throw a monkey wrench into the works and get you sidelined for months. The U.S. has immigration quotas, and if you get shuffled to the back of the line, you may not get a visa, understand?"

"But, sir, the Rabbi was our tent mate. So was Mendel, and now they are both dead. Will they not want to question us?"

The Chief shrugged. "Probably, but I already put the word out that you were with me until about midnight working on the drawings of the field hospital."

I frowned, as did Hans, "Why would you do that?"

"Look, fellas, I know that you didn't kill the Rabbi or the Mendel kid, but this new investigator doesn't know you guys like I do. See, fellas, there have been just a few too many deaths here in this camp. The U.S. Government doesn't run this camp, at least not like the one across the road, but they're responsible for security here. So they sent this Colonel Bain here. He's a hardass from the states, been in Washington for the war."

Chief Hawk patted my knee, "Now he's here to oversee the trial of those Nazi bastards across the road, but since we've got 'em locked up pretty tight, the Colonel will probably think he'd better take a look-see here first."

Hans asked, "How close a lookee, Chief?"

"Look-see, kid, look-see!" The Chief chuckled. "I don't expect too close. He doesn't have much of a staff yet." He stood and turned to the two of us. "I think it would be best if you guys made yourselves scarce."

I understood what he was saying. "Do you think we could move our gear in here, sir?"

"Don't see why not. After all, you guys work here, don't you?" Then he asked the question I had been waiting for, "You boys do want to go to America, don't you?"

In unison we answered, "Oh, yes, sir."

I guess we did. "Come Hans, let us retrieve our goods from the tent." We quickly ran to our tent. After packing our meager belongings in the pillow sacks, we stood for a minute looking down at Mendel's and the Rabbi's beds. Hans took the Bible from the Rabbi's end table, kissed it, then put it in his sack. Of Mendel's, we took nothing. We would hold Mendel in our hearts.

CHAPTER 31
Hans' Story

I was in much pain seeing Reb Horowitz dead. He was a good man, and I was proud to call him my friend. Now he and Mendel are gone and I wonder who will be next. Will it be Herschel or me?

Once Herschel and I had moved our belongings to the new building, we went back to work with our men. I wonder why the Chief Hawk wanted us to move into this building instead of staying in our tent or another tent.

There was carpentry work on the end of the building and then electrical wiring which we were eager to learn. We met a man from Bulgaria named Boris, who said he was an electrical man and used to run his own company. He and Herschel found three more men, a Pole, Filip from Gdansk,; a German Jew, Moishe, who came from the horrors of Auschwitz, and an Austrian who said he hid Jews from the Nazis, a farmer, whose wife and daughter were killed by a misdropped bomb one year ago. I don't remember his name now. They all had performed wiring of buildings and agreed to allow Herschel and me to work alongside them.

We worked hard this day, trying to forget the Rabbi's death, or at least try to put it behind us. We unreeled wire, nailed in metal electrical boxes and drilled holes in wooden wall supports, called studs. By late afternoon, we were exhausted.

We sat in the shade and shared a glass bottle filled with cool water. A shadow fell on me and I lifted my eyes. Maria stood before me and held out a hand, which I gripped and hauled myself to my feet. My, that woman was strong.

"Hans, we must talk."

"Ya, we must. Come, let us go into another room." I kept her hand in mine, and we walked away. Behind me, I saw Herschel grinning as he took another long drink of water.

We went into one of the storerooms, and I tried to pull her into my arms, but Maria put her hands on my chest and held me away. "Hans, this must end now." She crossed her arms across her chest. She looked sterner than I had ever seen her.

"What do you mean, Maria?"

"Hans, I can no longer be with you. I am frightened." She hugged herself. "You are surrounded by death." She was quivering now and sobbing softly, the tears running down her cheeks in rivulets.

Once more I reached for her but she threw her hands up and spun around, walking in small circles. "No, no. Oh, my Hans, I want to but I cannot." Her agony was palpable. She gripped handfuls of her hair and shook her head violently. The sobs grew louder and deeper.

I stood straight and gripped her by the shoulders, "I have been surrounded by death for a long time. I had hoped to put it all behind me."

Maria wrenched herself free. "But it follows you, Hans, and I want no part of it. I do not want it to touch me." She was near hysterics now, and I could see that I would not be able to talk to her

"We will speak perhaps tomorrow, when you have calmed down." I turned and walked away.

It was the beginning of the end. Now there was only Herschel and me. At least we had that.

We buried the Rabbi the next morning in the small wood behind the women's camp. It was well attended, and both Herschel and I spoke well of him. Many men came forward and spoke, and no one had anything but good things to say of that fine man. He probably would have been embarrassed by the accolades. I will be remembering him in the Kaddish all the years of my life.

One week later, Mr. Nowicki informed Herschel and me that his family had agreed to sponsor us. Although we were apprehensive, the thought of a new life and a new family was a comfort.

I tried to see Miss Maria several times but she was either out or her assistant informed me that she was unavailable. Two months later Herschel and I boarded a ship in Antwerp and left for Chicago, America.

I never did have that talk with Maria and did not know what became of her. That is, until one day, two years later, Herschel and I were working on an apartment remodel with Mr. Nowicki's brother, Daniel, in the city of Chicago, USA. I was holding a sheet of plywood against a wall and felt a tap on my shoulder.

"Hey, you. Have you got a minute for an old friend?" said Miss Maria.

I thought I recognized the voice and turned around slowly. Yes, it was she. I lowered the sheet of plywood and held out my arms. She jumped into them. And that's how my wife, your Aunt Maria, came back into my life. Six months later we married and your father, Herschel, was my best man, of course.

Life goes on.

Epilogue

So there you have it, my children, the story of your Uncle Hans and me, up until the time we came to America. What happened after that, you already know. How we met our wives, your mother and your Aunt Maria, our work and schooling, where we lived and all the rest. We never lied to you, not really. Whenever you asked about our pasts, we just didn't go into details, if you remember.

I also know that you once asked why we mumbled when we worked. You, Ancel, who worked with us, always wanted to know what we were saying. Oh, it was great fun spinning yarns each time you asked. But now I will tell you. We were saying the Kaddish over and over as a way of asking forgiveness for the friends who were killed, for the thousands of men, women and children we saw gassed and then heaped on our little trolleys and dumped in the pits to be burned or just buried; and mostly for Rabbi Horowitz and Mendel. I'd made it into a little song, and sometimes we sang it or just hummed.

Did you really want us to tell you the details? Did you want me to tell you that each morning I prayed that none of my children would ever experience the horrors I and your Uncle Hans saw, lived, experienced? Now I go to my rest peacefully, knowing that the world is different, that you and your children will be safe.

Do I have any regrets? Yes, of course, I wouldn't be human if I didn't. I regret that you never got to meet my real brother, Isaac, my parents, my sister Miriam, and especially Rabbi Horowitz and my friend Mendel. I think you would have liked them.

You may wonder why a couple of good Jews like Hans and I never went to Israel, even for a visit. We couldn't. It would have been too painful, and we didn't want to live in the past. The greatest thing that ever happened to us was being taken in by the Nowickis. They were our American family. That is why we have always stayed in touch with them, why you played with their children and why we sat on the board of their foundation.

Now, do you tell your cousins this story? Hans says no. I say yes. You are all our children and we raised you to be strong, independent people. We leave it in your capable hands. Both Hans and I loved you all deeply, and we will miss seeing your smiling faces. Have good lives and leave this world a better place than when you arrived.

Your loving Father and your Uncle.

*　　　　*　　　　*

"Well. Do you think its all true?" asked Miriam.

"I guess. Don't know why they'd have written it all down just to bullshit us," said Sammy. "What do you think, Al?"

Al was sprawled on the old leather sofa in Mim's den, sipping a cup of tea, letting the steam envelop his face. Sammy sat on the edge of the recliner fiddling with his coffee and Mim just looked beat, haggard, like she was just lost. "I don't know, Sammy, what do you guys think? I mean, I believe the story, though it's going to take me a while to process it all, but do we tell Nate and Ruthie?" They were our cousins, Hans' children.

"I can't, Al. If we do decide, you'll have to do it," whispered Miriam.

"Yeah, man. I hate to say it but it's on you now. I've got to get back to Vegas anyway. I'm on duty tomorrow night." Sammy was the ultimate buck passer. Nothing was ever his fault.

Well, I was the boss of a good-sized construction company, used to hiring and firing, dealing out bad and good news, just like my dad and uncle. "O.K., I'll handle it. I'll decide. I saw them at Pop's funeral, so I know they're still in town. Let me think on it a while."

And that's where I'll leave it. Two years have passed since Pop's death. I still say Kaddish for the old man and Uncle Hans and for all the others who have died. Will I pass this manuscript on to my kids? I don't know. Maybe its time to just let the past die.

The End

MISSING PIECES

by Don Kafrissen

Following is a sample of Don Kafrissen's next exciting book.

To what lengths will a man go to protect his intellectual property and insure its safe delivery? Especially when he employs others to make the trip? As it turns out, Dave and Chris Manley don't even know what they are carrying!

PROLOGUE

The FEDEX truck pulled to a hasty stop in front of the casino. The woman driver was running late and dashed to the front door, slamming the self-locking van door behind her. As she entered the neon-lit lobby, a tall man, also in a FEDEX uniform strode swiftly to the driver's door. With a quick glance around, he easily picked the lock and entered. In less than a minute, he emerged from the back carrying a small package under his arm.

He immediately walked over to a dark sedan, climbed in and drove away. Several blocks away, the sedan pulled over to the curb. If anyone was watching, they would have heard a loud bang and seen the car fill with smoke. The tall man opened the door and rolled onto the dark sidewalk coughing and vomiting. The contents of the parcel were melted beyond recognition. In fact, a large, black hole was burned into the seat. The thin man dreaded returning to his employer, Mr. Hammond, with his report. Mr. Hammond was not an easy man to please and took bad news poorly. He was sometimes known to expend his wrath on the messenger, rather than the message.

However, the tall man survived his encounter, the package bringing him no more than a violently upset stomach for a few days and his report to the aforementioned Mr. Hammond resulting in no more than a stern dressing down and a black eye. The thin man considered himself lucky. In fact, his luck was running out. His next assignment was to intercept a courier carrying a similar package.

The thin man glanced at the color-fax photo in his hand as he stood near the gate of the American Airlines concourse at McCarron Airport in Las Vegas two weeks later. The black eye was healed and his stomach was now full of linguini with clam sauce. Another glance and he selected his man. The target was a man of medium height, sandy hair and a Tom Selleck mustache. He wore a lightweight gabardine suit and a white on white shirt with a blue tie with small polka dots. The thin man estimated his age at about 40, give or take a couple of years. He appeared to be in good condition and, of course, wouldn't be wearing a gun. The courier looked neither right nor left and strode toward the baggage claim area, forsaking the moving sidewalks. The thin man didn't and easily stayed abreast, sometimes even getting somewhat ahead. He also noted that the courier was carrying a slim metal briefcase with combination locks and that a thin stainless steel cable ran up the man's right coat sleeve.

The thin man stayed half dozen paces behind the courier at the baggage claim. The courier only reclaimed a small duffel bag and strode outside. Just as they reached the door to the taxi stand, the thin man bumped against the courier.

"Oh, excuse me. I just wasn't watching where I was going."

"That's alright. I was just getting a cab downtown," the courier replied smiling.

"Are you going down to the strip?" asked the thin man, referring to the main Las Vegas avenue containing most of the lavish hotels.

"Why, yes, I'm staying at the Stardust just for the night."

"Why don't we share? I've got a cab waiting. A friend was supposed to come in on a flight this evening and never showed up," suggested the thin man, gently taking the courier's arm.

With only a second's hesitation, the courier said, "Sure, sounds O.K. to me." Which was unfortunate as he was a new courier and not conversant with all the rules of courier-hood. The first being Never, Never travel with anyone, anywhere until you've disposed of the package. In courierese, all deliveries are the "Package."

"Here, let me get that for you," the thin man expertly tossed the duffel bag in the trunk and opened the rear door. The courier smiled his thanks and got in, holding the briefcase on his lap.

The cab got underway and the two men in the rear engaged in small talk about Las Vegas in general and the casinos in particular. The thin man neglected to give the driver a destination and the courier thought it odd, but assumed the driver was taking him back to his starting point.

The next thing the courier knew, the thin man had extracted a small automatic pistol from his coat pocket and shoved it in the courier's ribs. "Give me the briefcase, my friend."

Naturally, the courier was somewhat upset and pointed helplessly to the cable attached to the briefcase. The thin man shrugged and tapped on the divider window with the gun barrel. He held up the briefcase and cable for the cabby to see. The cabby nodded, indicating that he understood.

At the next exit, as they were getting near the city, the cab exited and drove away from the lights. The courier thought that he ought to make an attempt to get away. He inched his hand toward the door handle and looked over his left shoulder, hoping to distract his seatmate even momentarily.

The thin man shook his head in disgust. "Don't even think about it, my friend. You'll get your chance soon enough. The courier relaxed and sat back. After all, they wanted the package, not him. His orders were to give up the package, always.

Soon, the lights faded behind them and they were speeding out toward the dry, pale desert. A few moments later, the cab coasted to a halt, two wheels off the side of the road. The cab driver just sat still, hands on the wheel.

"Unbutton your shirt," the thin man gestured with the gun.

Having no other option, the courier did as he was told. The thin, shiny cable exited the shirt sleeve and trailed down over his chest and encircled his waist, coming together in an elaborate digital push-button lock, a green LED pulsing faintly.

"I don't suppose they told you the combination," asked the thin man. The courier just shook his head.

"They never do. Policy, you know."

The thin man nodded thoughtfully. "The briefcase?"

The courier looked at him apologetically, "Stainless mesh inside."

"And the pulsating light? Probably monitoring your heartbeat?"

The courier shrugged, he didn't know. The light pulsed on, off, on, off.

Finally the thin man made up his mind. "I guess we'll have to give it a try. Would you mind rolling your window down?" He inclined his head toward the handle.

The courier complied and the summer heat crawled into the car, looking for a place to cool down.

"Now hold your right hand up, letting a few inches of cable dangle from your sleeve." The courier did as he was told and tried to draw away from his arm as if it were someone else's. The thin man held up the pistol and fired a shot severing the cable, the bullet passing harmlessly out the open window and digging up a furrow in the desert sand.

As the shot boomed in the narrow confines of the car, the courier closed his eyes and grimaced.

The briefcase fell into his lap. The cable just dangled. The LED turned red and a thin, high whine came from the box on his chest. He clawed at it, trying to slip out but the cable allowed not enough slack. He looked at the thin man and started to cry, wetting his pants at the same time. The thin man snatched the briefcase to his chest and lurched for the door. Just then the courier made a grab for the thin man's coat. He pulled the briefcase from his grasp just as it went off. The narrow cord of Semtex explosive blew the thin man's arm off at the shoulder and nearly severed the courier's head. The explosion of blood and body matter sprayed the dividing window and some came through the sliding window, catching the driver in the back of the neck. Before he knew it, he was out the door and on his knees on the macadam. There were no other cars in sight.

A fine, blue smoke came through the open window. Carefully the cabby opened the rear driver's side door. The thin man was still alive, but the shoulder socket was gushing blood. The thin man looked stupidly at his arm, lying across the courier's lap. "Can you help me?" he pleaded with the cabby.

"Sure," said the cabby, a small man named Ronnie. He reached down on the floor and retrieved the pistol. He held it against the thin man's temple and pulled the trigger. The small caliber automatic made a popping sound, muffled as it was against the now smoking temple. The thin man jerked once and was quiet, head now against the back of the seat. Ronnie guessed he'd have to tell Mr. Hammond the bad news this time. If he was lucky, he'd get off with only a black eye, too, but somehow he doubted it.

After wiping the steering wheel and gun, which he placed back in the thin man's left hand, he started back down the highway. He had quite a walk to the nearest phone, but it was a nice night and he had a lot of thinking to do. Mr. Hammond surely wanted the package that the courier was carrying but sometimes he just didn't understand the complexities of the job.

* * *

About the author:

Don Kafrissen lives on five rural acres on Florida's West Coast with his wife Diane, 2 cats, and a dog. He and his wife built their own house and are *car people*, taking part in many car shows and cruise-ins each year with their vintage autos. Don started the Brooksville Writers' Group several years ago and now enjoys friendships with many local authors.

Don is a veteran of the U.S. Navy, has lived in Rhode Island, Canada, Texas, California, Vermont and many other places. He has visited 43 different countries and he and his wife once lived 10 years on a 40' Endeavour sailboat, spending many happy months in the Caribbean.

Don is semi-retired and owns a power tool repair business and a publishing company. He is a graduate of Cranston High School East in Cranston, R.I. and Queen's University's McArthur College in Kingston, Ontario.

His Bucket List still includes a trip to Ireland and to the Burning Man Festival.

82574139R00124

Made in the USA
Columbia, SC
18 December 2017